Henry Van Dyke, Howard Pyle

The first Christmas tree

Henry Van Dyke, Howard Pyle

The first Christmas tree

ISBN/EAN: 9783741193811

Manufactured in Europe, USA, Canada, Australia, Japa

Cover: Foto ©Andreas Hilbeck / pixelio.de

Manufactured and distributed by brebook publishing software
(www.brebook.com)

Henry Van Dyke, Howard Pyle

The first Christmas tree

THE FIRST CHRISTMAS TREE. A STORY OF THE FOREST

THE FIRST
CHRISTMAS-
TREE
BY HENRY
VAN DYKE
ILLVSTRA-
TED BY HOW-
ARD PYLE

CHARLES SCRIBNER'S SONS
NEW YORK MDCCCXCVII

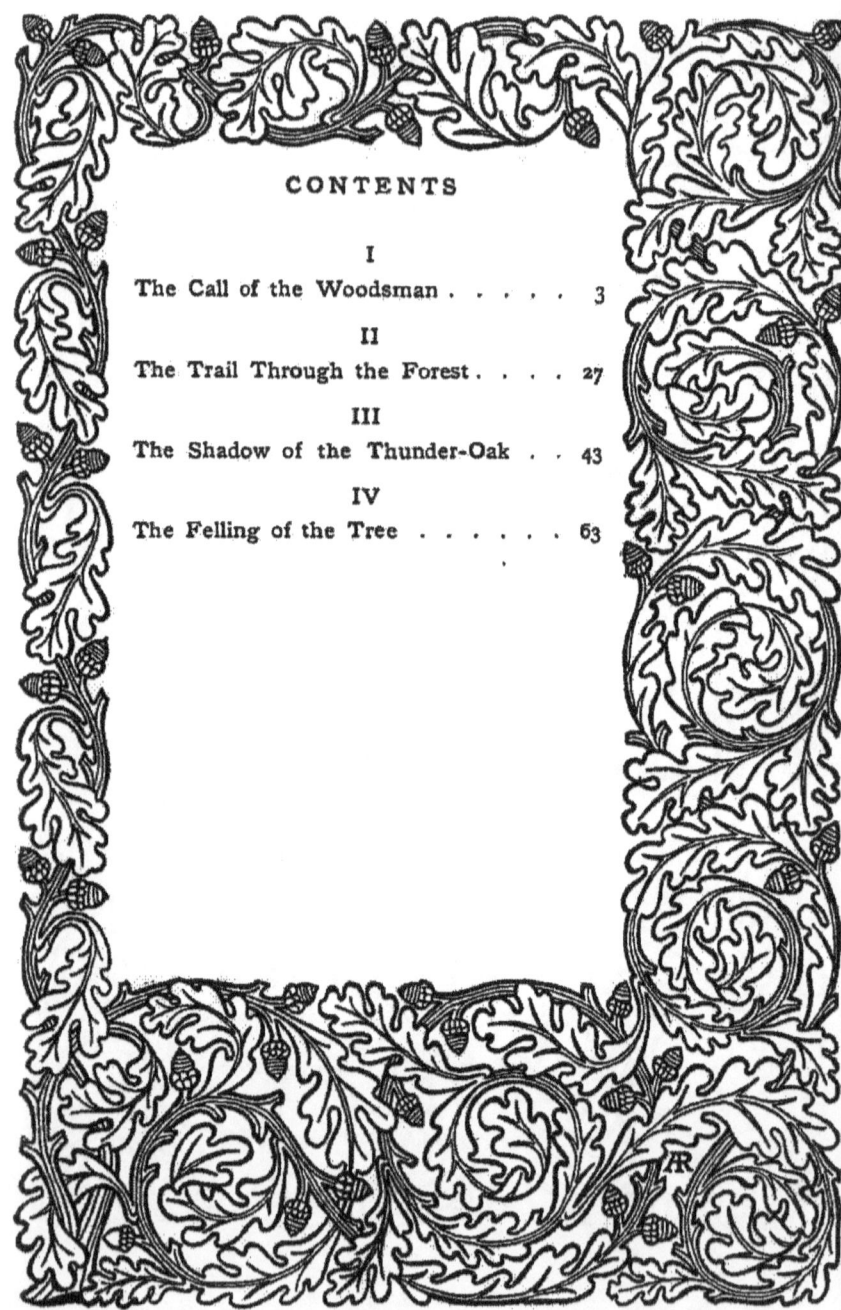

CONTENTS

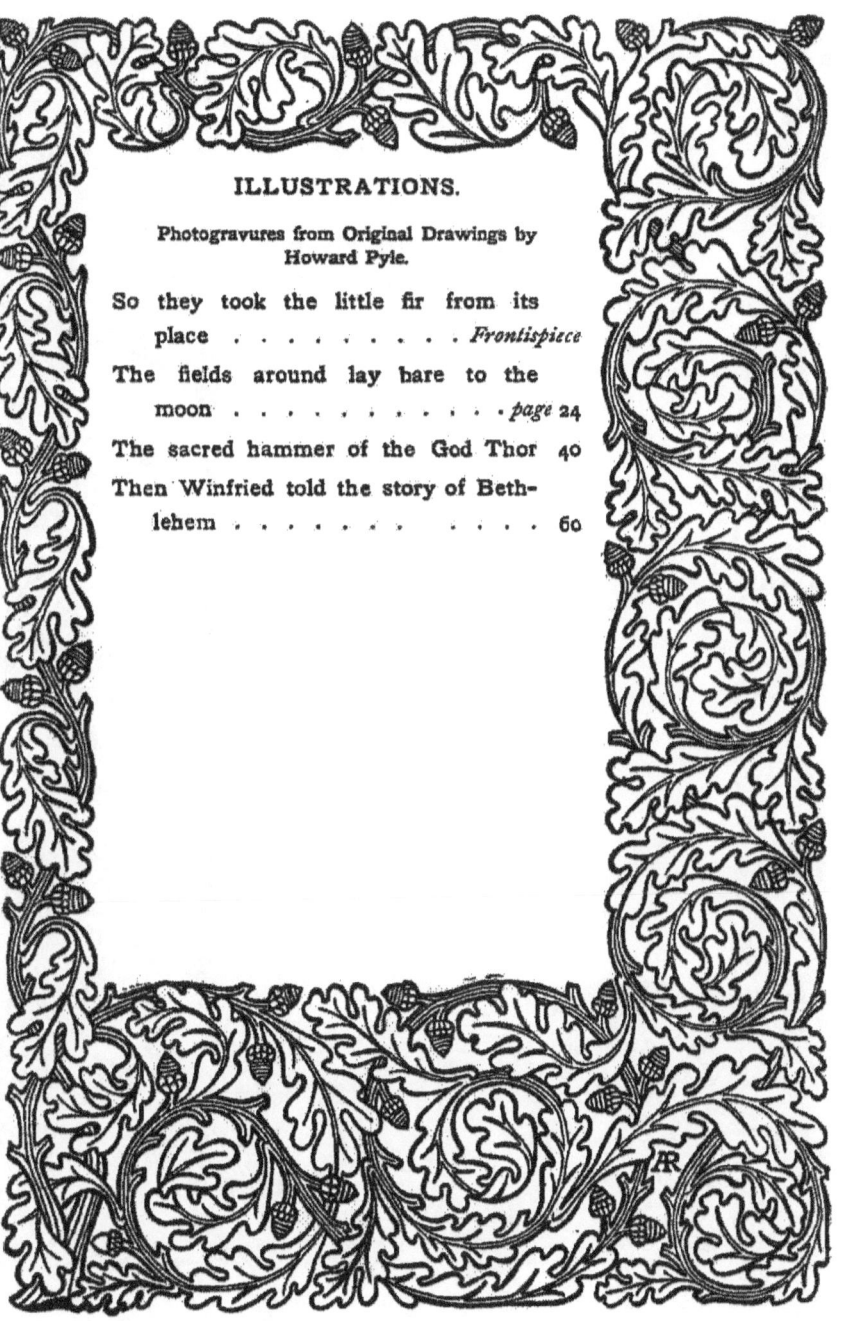

ILLUSTRATIONS.

Photogravures from Original Drawings by
Howard Pyle.

I

THE CALL OF THE WOODSMAN

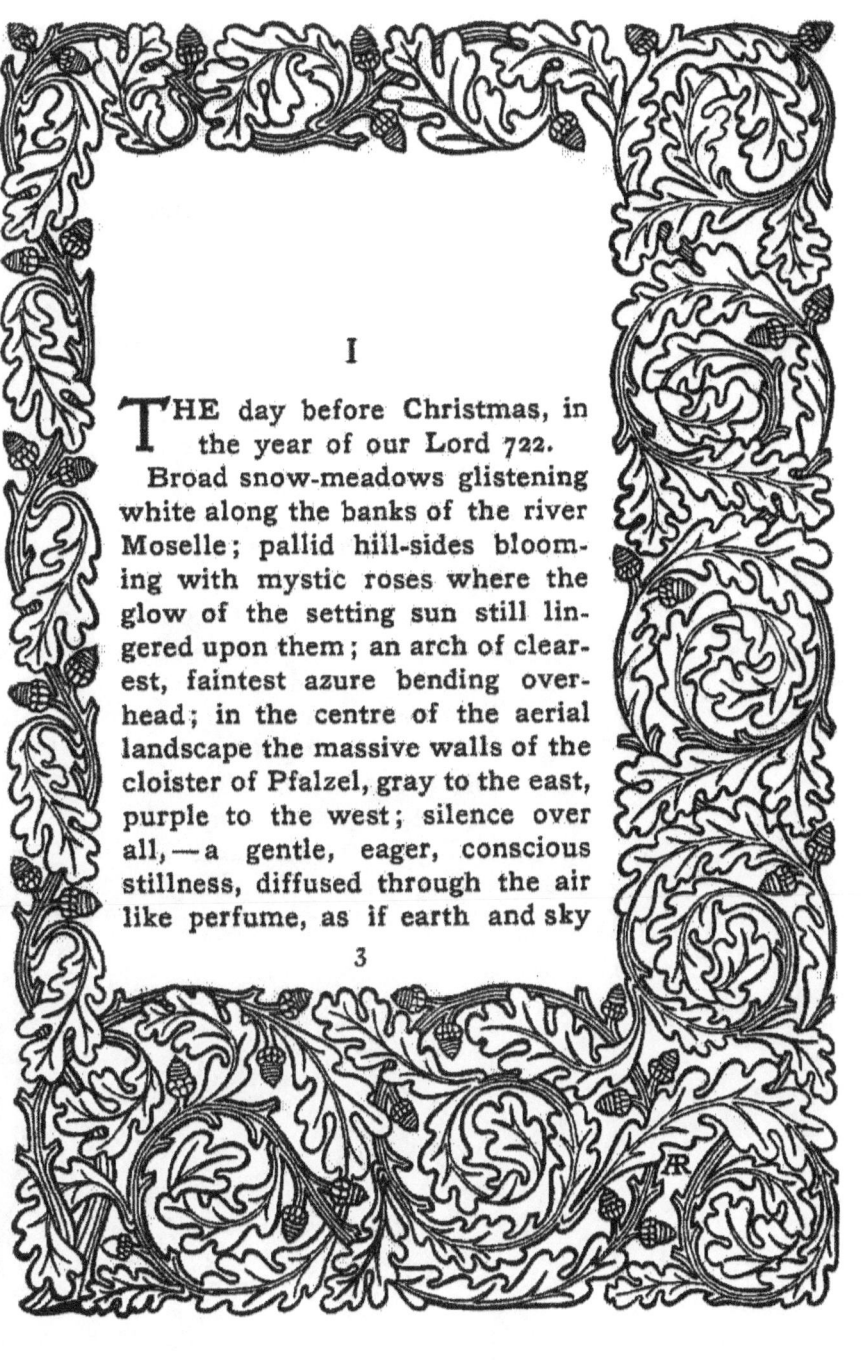

I

THE day before Christmas, in the year of our Lord 722.

Broad snow-meadows glistening white along the banks of the river Moselle; pallid hill-sides blooming with mystic roses where the glow of the setting sun still lingered upon them; an arch of clearest, faintest azure bending overhead; in the centre of the aerial landscape the massive walls of the cloister of Pfalzel, gray to the east, purple to the west; silence over all,—a gentle, eager, conscious stillness, diffused through the air like perfume, as if earth and sky

3

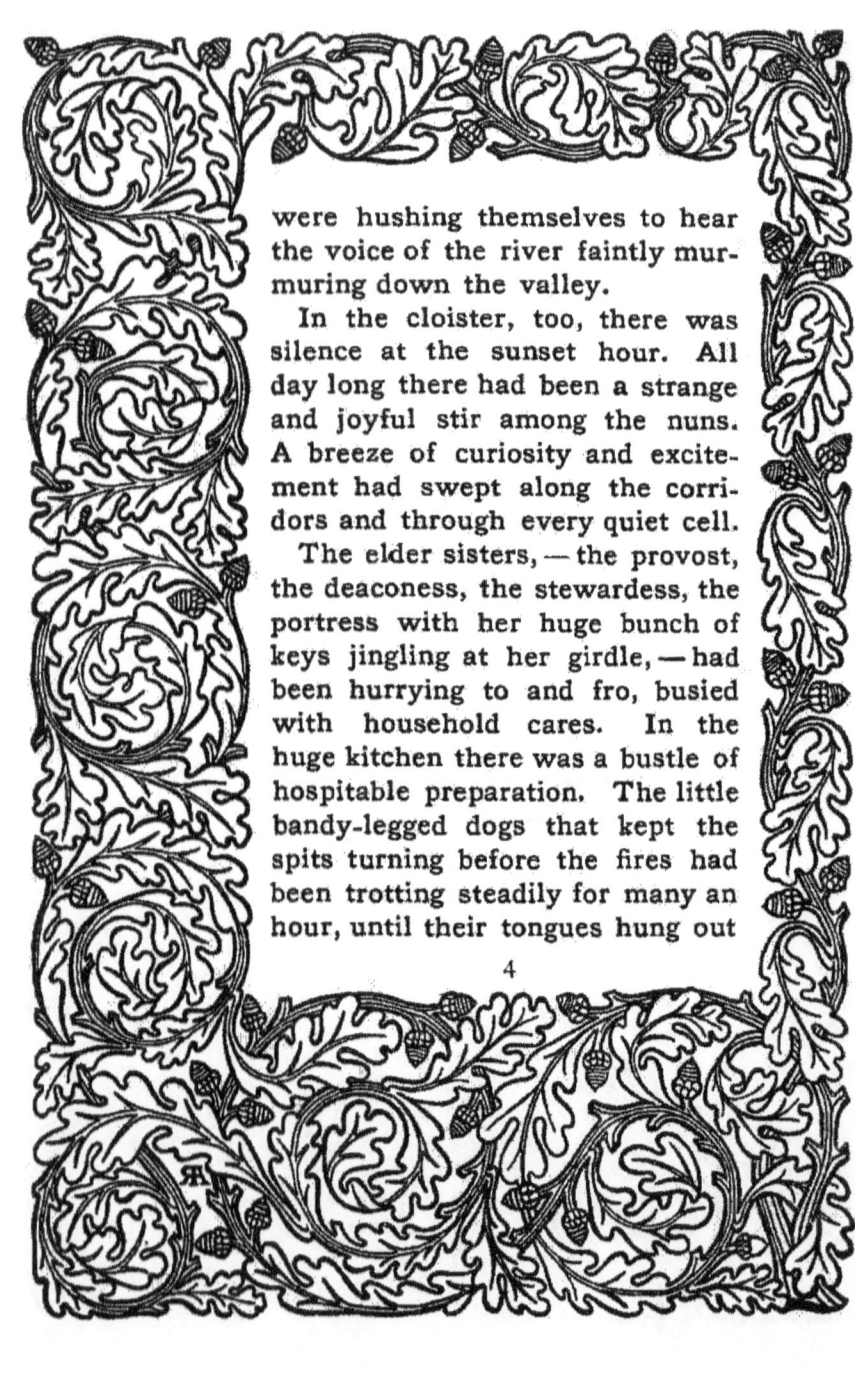

were hushing themselves to hear
the voice of the river faintly murmuring down the valley.

In the cloister, too, there was
silence at the sunset hour. All
day long there had been a strange
and joyful stir among the nuns.
A breeze of curiosity and excite-
ment had swept along the corridors and through every quiet cell.

The elder sisters, — the provost,
the deaconess, the stewardess, the
portress with her huge bunch of
keys jingling at her girdle, — had
been hurrying to and fro, busied
with household cares. In the
huge kitchen there was a bustle of
hospitable preparation. The little
bandy-legged dogs that kept the
spits turning before the fires had
been trotting steadily for many an
hour, until their tongues hung out

4

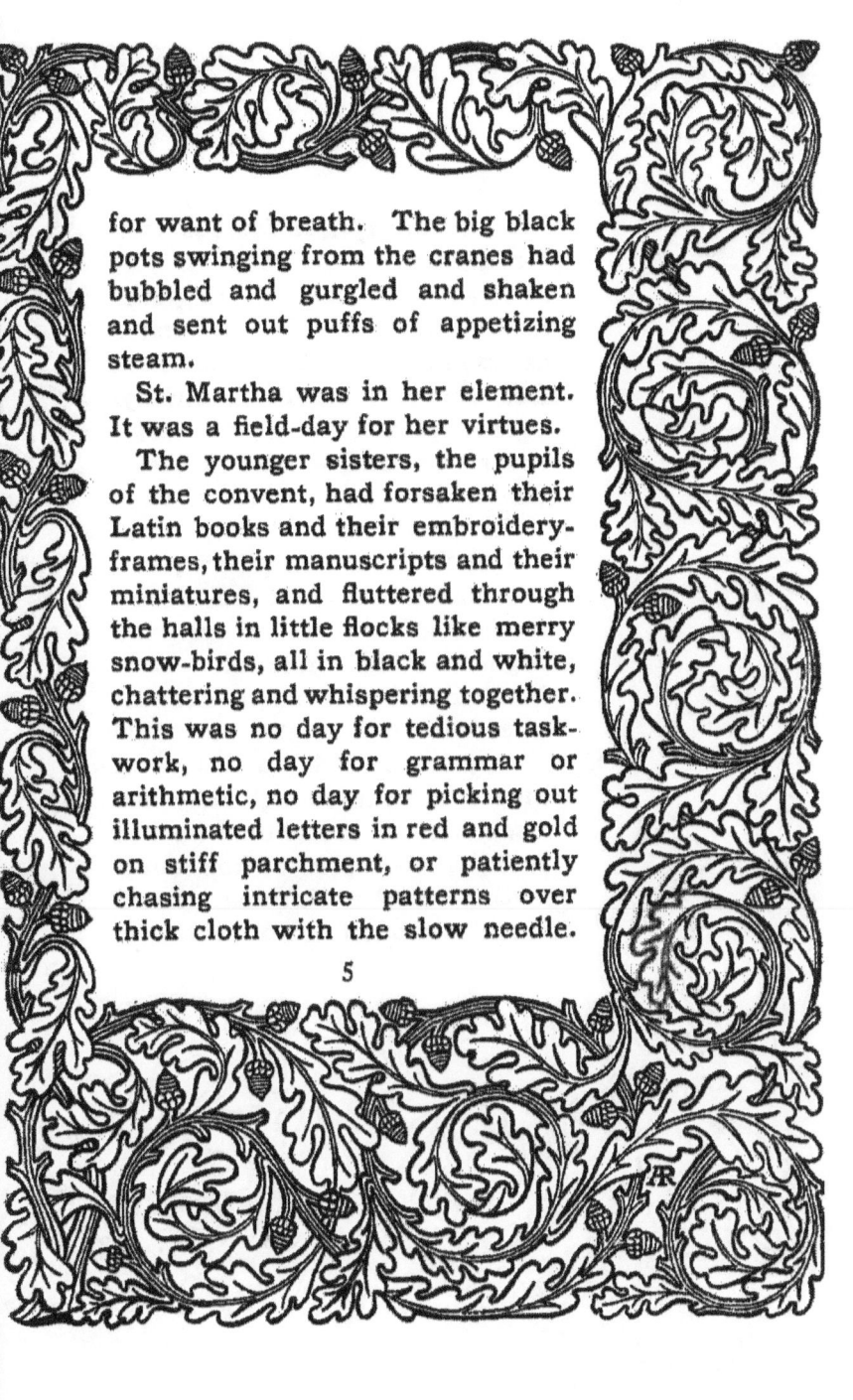

for want of breath. The big black
pots swinging from the cranes had
bubbled and gurgled and shaken
and sent out puffs of appetizing
steam.

St. Martha was in her element.
It was a field-day for her virtues.

The younger sisters, the pupils
of the convent, had forsaken their
Latin books and their embroidery-
frames, their manuscripts and their
miniatures, and fluttered through
the halls in little flocks like merry
snow-birds, all in black and white,
chattering and whispering together.
This was no day for tedious task-
work, no day for grammar or
arithmetic, no day for picking out
illuminated letters in red and gold
on stiff parchment, or patiently
chasing intricate patterns over
thick cloth with the slow needle.

5

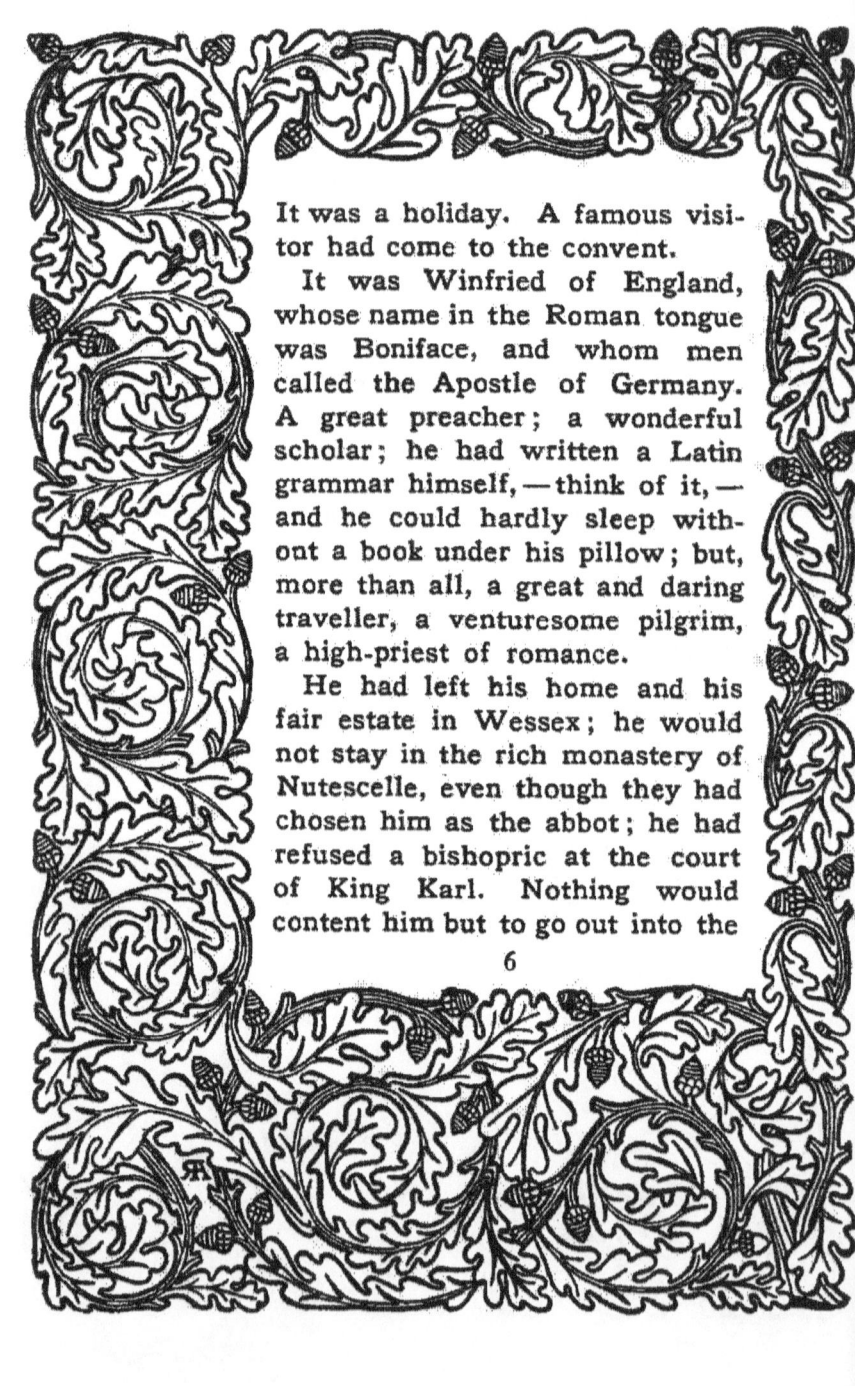

It was a holiday. A famous visitor had come to the convent.

It was Winfried of England, whose name in the Roman tongue was Boniface, and whom men called the Apostle of Germany. A great preacher; a wonderful scholar; he had written a Latin grammar himself, — think of it, — and he could hardly sleep without a book under his pillow; but, more than all, a great and daring traveller, a venturesome pilgrim, a high-priest of romance.

He had left his home and his fair estate in Wessex; he would not stay in the rich monastery of Nutescelle, even though they had chosen him as the abbot; he had refused a bishopric at the court of King Karl. Nothing would content him but to go out into the

6

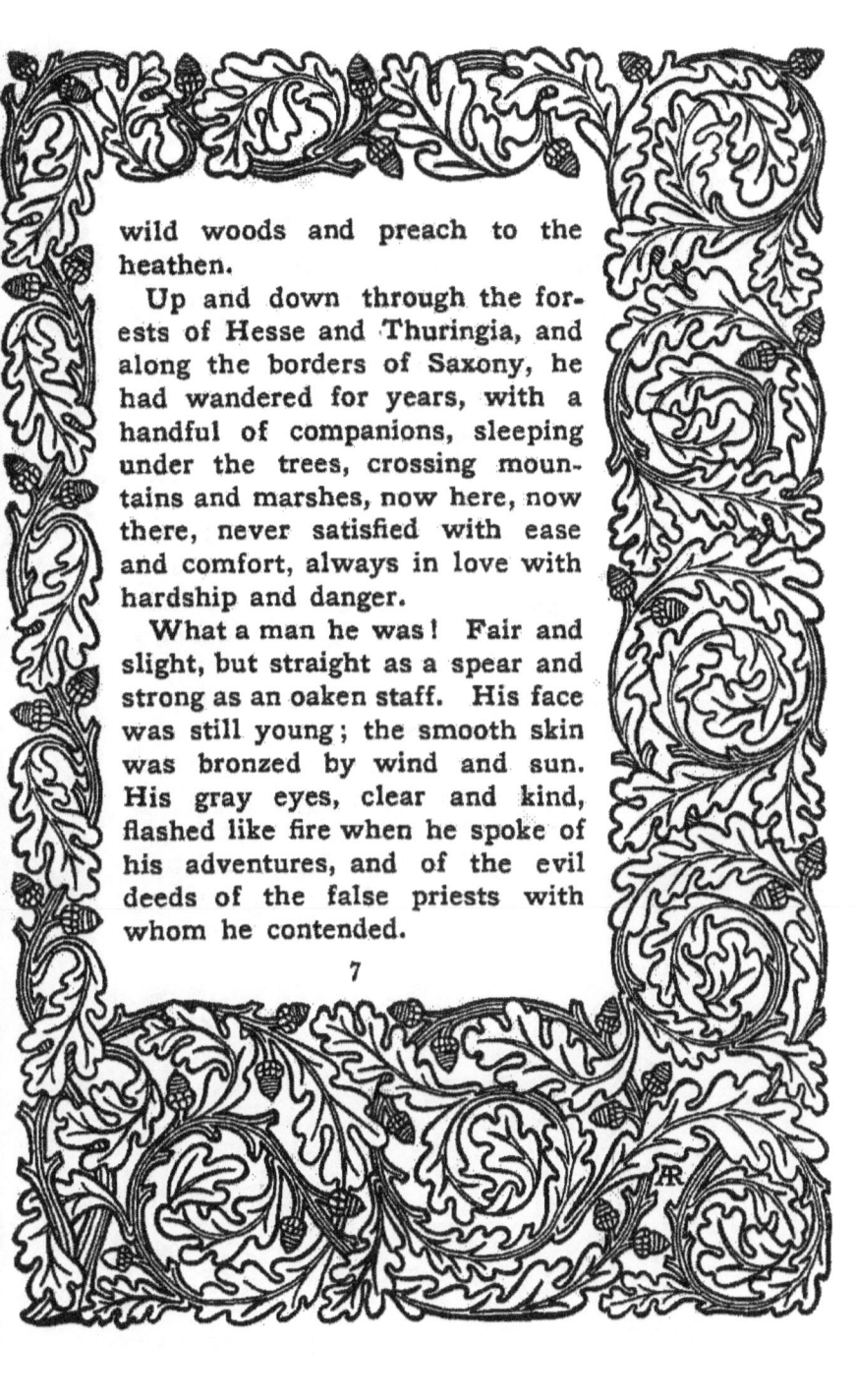

wild woods and preach to the
heathen.

Up and down through the forests of Hesse and Thuringia, and
along the borders of Saxony, he
had wandered for years, with a
handful of companions, sleeping
under the trees, crossing moun-
tains and marshes, now here, now
there, never satisfied with ease
and comfort, always in love with
hardship and danger.

What a man he was! Fair and
slight, but straight as a spear and
strong as an oaken staff. His face
was still young; the smooth skin
was bronzed by wind and sun.
His gray eyes, clear and kind,
flashed like fire when he spoke of
his adventures, and of the evil
deeds of the false priests with
whom he contended.

7

What tales he had told that day! Not of miracles wrought by sacred relics; not of courts and councils and splendid cathedrals; though he knew much of these things, and had been at Rome and received the Pope's blessing. But today he had spoken of long journeyings by sea and land; of perils by fire and flood; of wolves and bears and fierce snowstorms and black nights in the lonely forest; of dark altars of heathen gods, and weird, bloody sacrifices, and narrow escapes from murderous bands of wandering savages.

The little novices had gathered around him, and their faces had grown pale and their eyes bright as they listened with parted lips, entranced in admiration, twining their arms about one another's

8

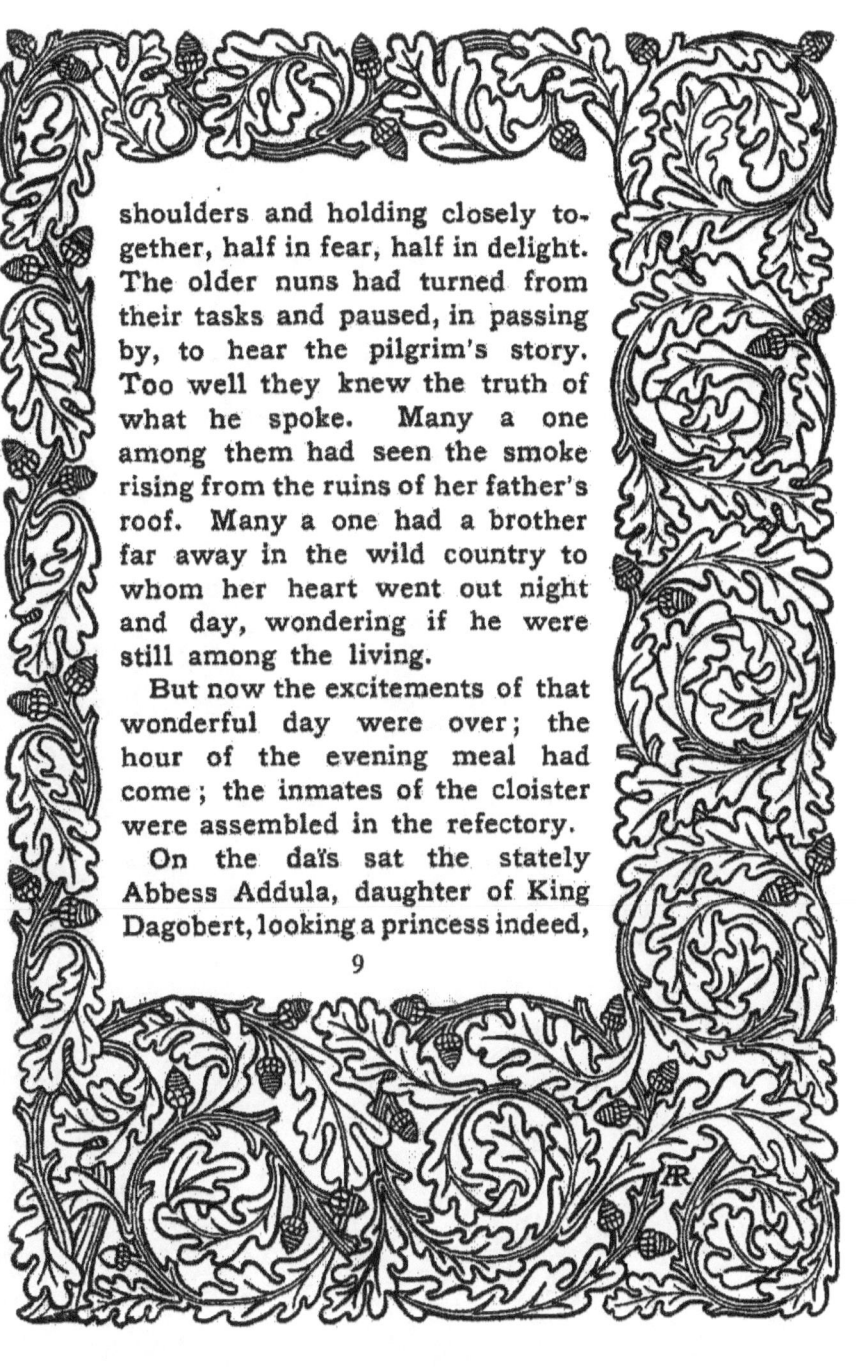

shoulders and holding closely together, half in fear, half in delight.
The older nuns had turned from
their tasks and paused, in passing
by, to hear the pilgrim's story.
Too well they knew the truth of
what he spoke. Many a one
among them had seen the smoke
rising from the ruins of her father's
roof. Many a one had a brother
far away in the wild country to
whom her heart went out night
and day, wondering if he were
still among the living.

But now the excitements of that
wonderful day were over; the
hour of the evening meal had
come; the inmates of the cloister
were assembled in the refectory.

On the daïs sat the stately
Abbess Addula, daughter of King
Dagobert, looking a princess indeed,

9

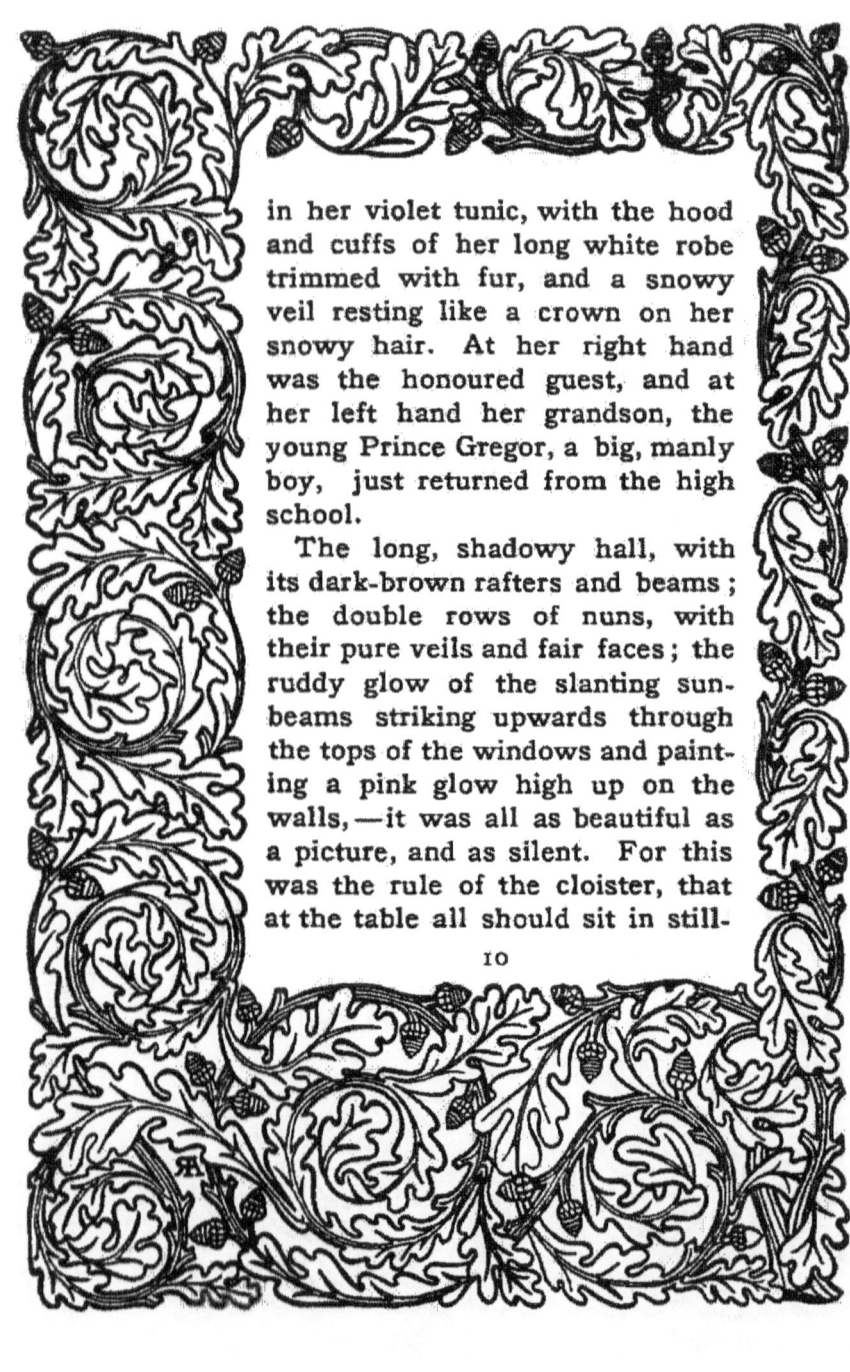

in her violet tunic, with the hood and cuffs of her long white robe trimmed with fur, and a snowy veil resting like a crown on her snowy hair. At her right hand was the honoured guest, and at her left hand her grandson, the young Prince Gregor, a big, manly boy, just returned from the high school.

The long, shadowy hall, with its dark-brown rafters and beams; the double rows of nuns, with their pure veils and fair faces; the ruddy glow of the slanting sunbeams striking upwards through the tops of the windows and painting a pink glow high up on the walls,—it was all as beautiful as a picture, and as silent. For this was the rule of the cloister, that at the table all should sit in still-

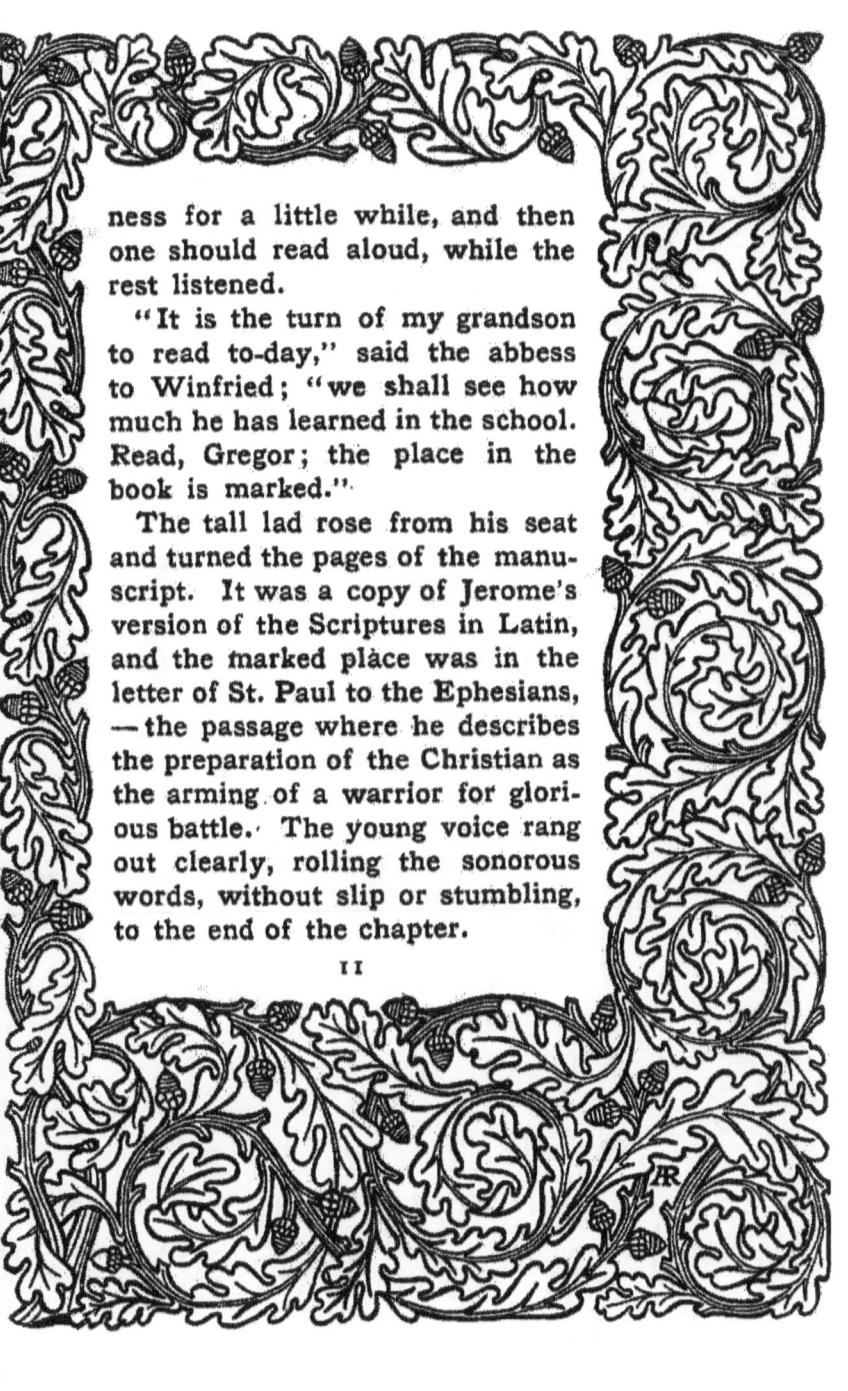

ness for a little while, and then one should read aloud, while the rest listened.

"It is the turn of my grandson to read to-day," said the abbess to Winfried; "we shall see how much he has learned in the school. Read, Gregor; the place in the book is marked."

The tall lad rose from his seat and turned the pages of the manuscript. It was a copy of Jerome's version of the Scriptures in Latin, and the marked place was in the letter of St. Paul to the Ephesians, —the passage where he describes the preparation of the Christian as the arming of a warrior for glorious battle. The young voice rang out clearly, rolling the sonorous words, without slip or stumbling, to the end of the chapter.

11

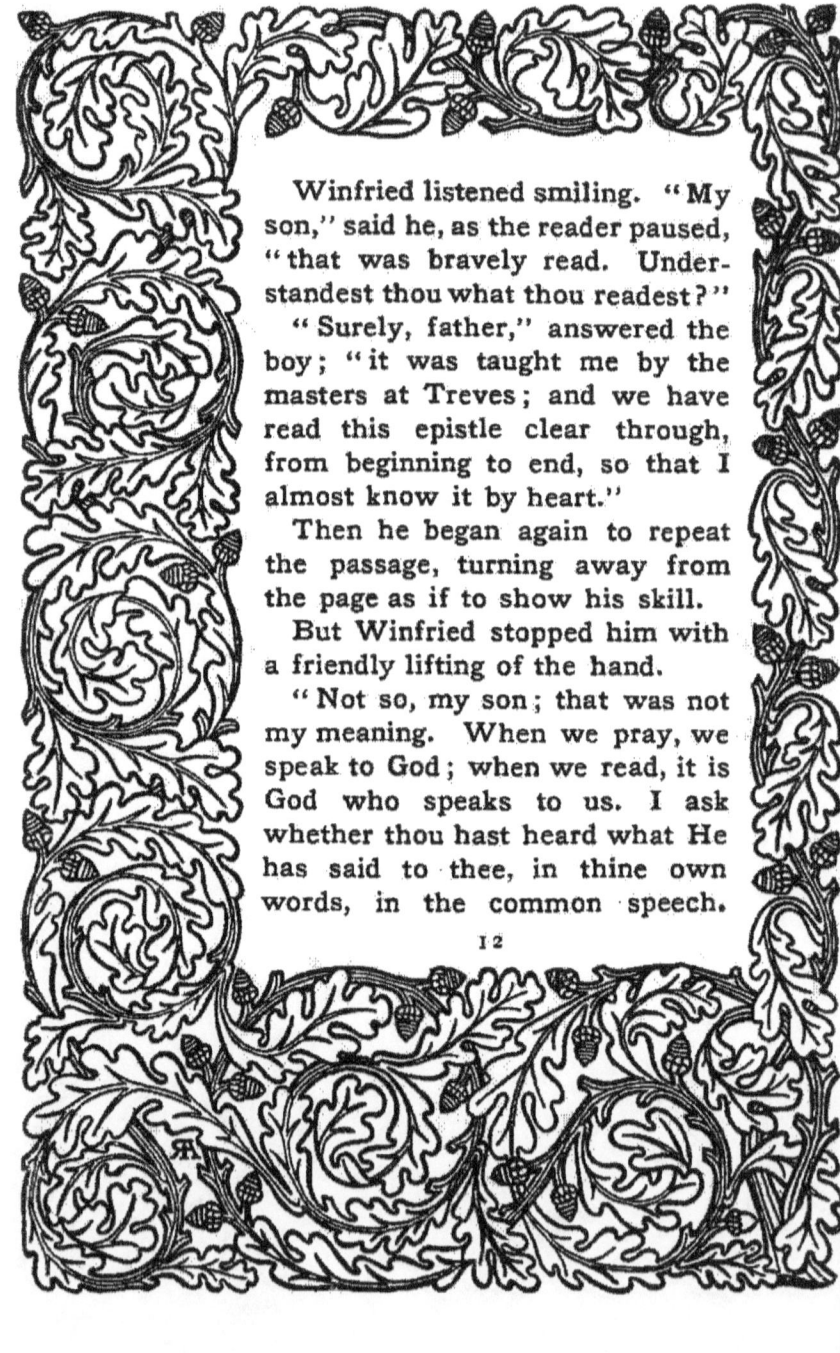

Winfried listened smiling. "My son," said he, as the reader paused, "that was bravely read. Understandest thou what thou readest?"

"Surely, father," answered the boy; "it was taught me by the masters at Treves; and we have read this epistle clear through, from beginning to end, so that I almost know it by heart."

Then he began again to repeat the passage, turning away from the page as if to show his skill.

But Winfried stopped him with a friendly lifting of the hand.

"Not so, my son; that was not my meaning. When we pray, we speak to God; when we read, it is God who speaks to us. I ask whether thou hast heard what He has said to thee, in thine own words, in the common speech.

12

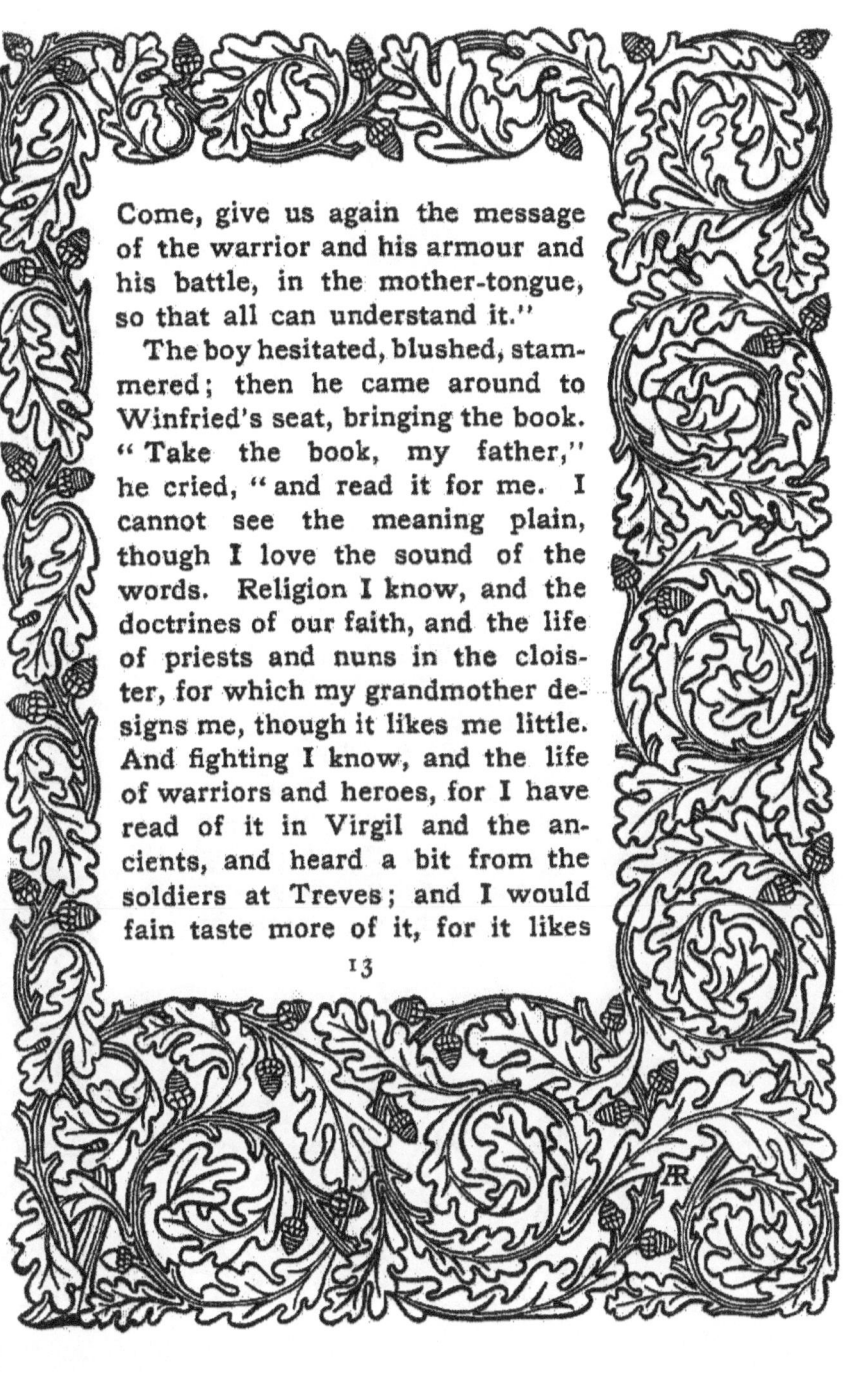

Come, give us again the message
of the warrior and his armour and
his battle, in the mother-tongue,
so that all can understand it."

The boy hesitated, blushed, stam-
mered; then he came around to
Winfried's seat, bringing the book.
"Take the book, my father,"
he cried, "and read it for me. I
cannot see the meaning plain,
though I love the sound of the
words. Religion I know, and the
doctrines of our faith, and the life
of priests and nuns in the cloister, for which my grandmother de-
signs me, though it likes me little.
And fighting I know, and the life
of warriors and heroes, for I have
read of it in Virgil and the an-
cients, and heard a bit from the
soldiers at Treves; and I would
fain taste more of it, for it likes

13

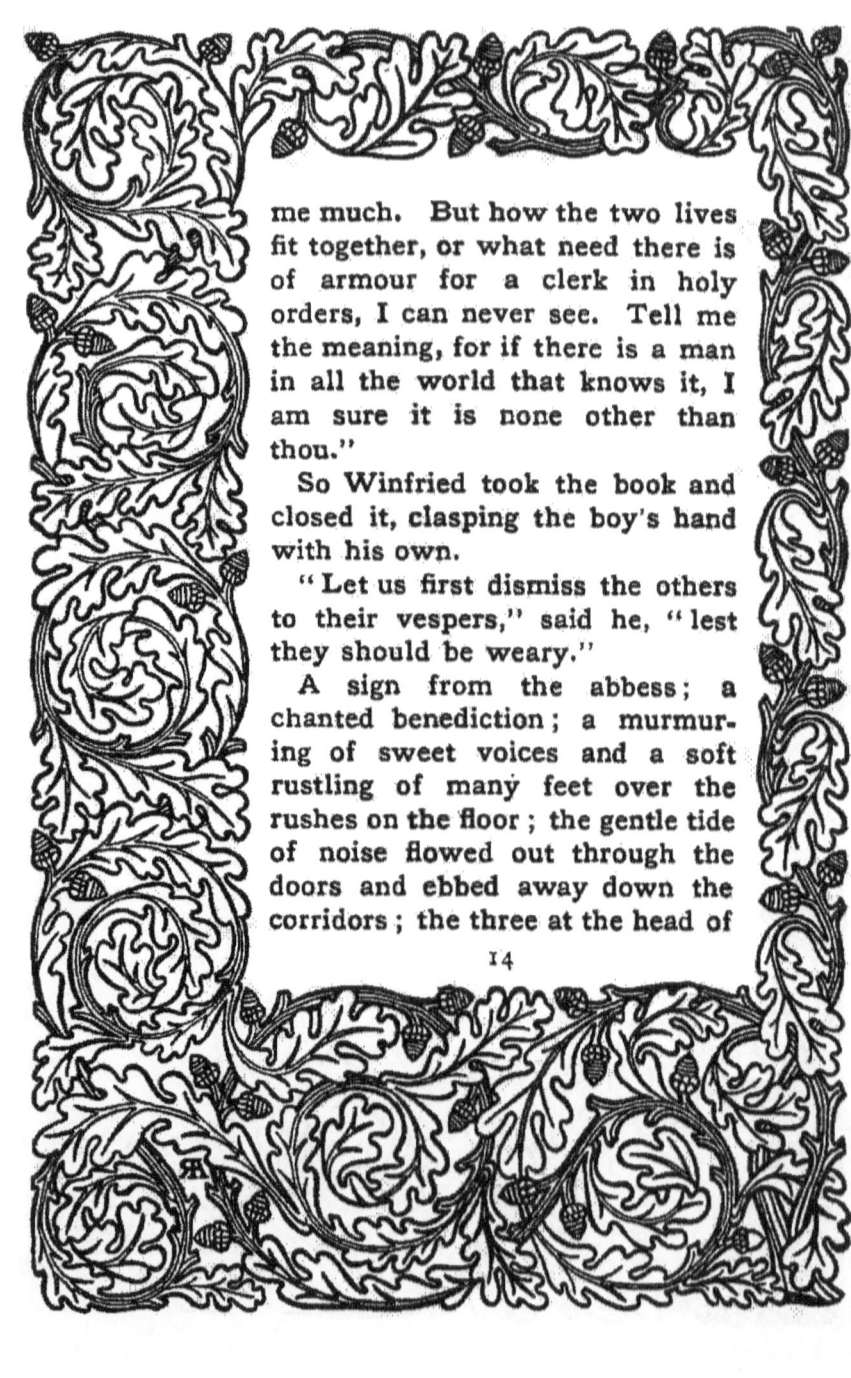

me much. But how the two lives
fit together, or what need there is
of armour for a clerk in holy
orders, I can never see. Tell me
the meaning, for if there is a man
in all the world that knows it, I
am sure it is none other than
thou."

So Winfried took the book and
closed it, clasping the boy's hand
with his own.

"Let us first dismiss the others
to their vespers," said he, "lest
they should be weary."

A sign from the abbess; a
chanted benediction; a murmuring of sweet voices and a soft
rustling of many feet over the
rushes on the floor; the gentle tide
of noise flowed out through the
doors and ebbed away down the
corridors; the three at the head of

14

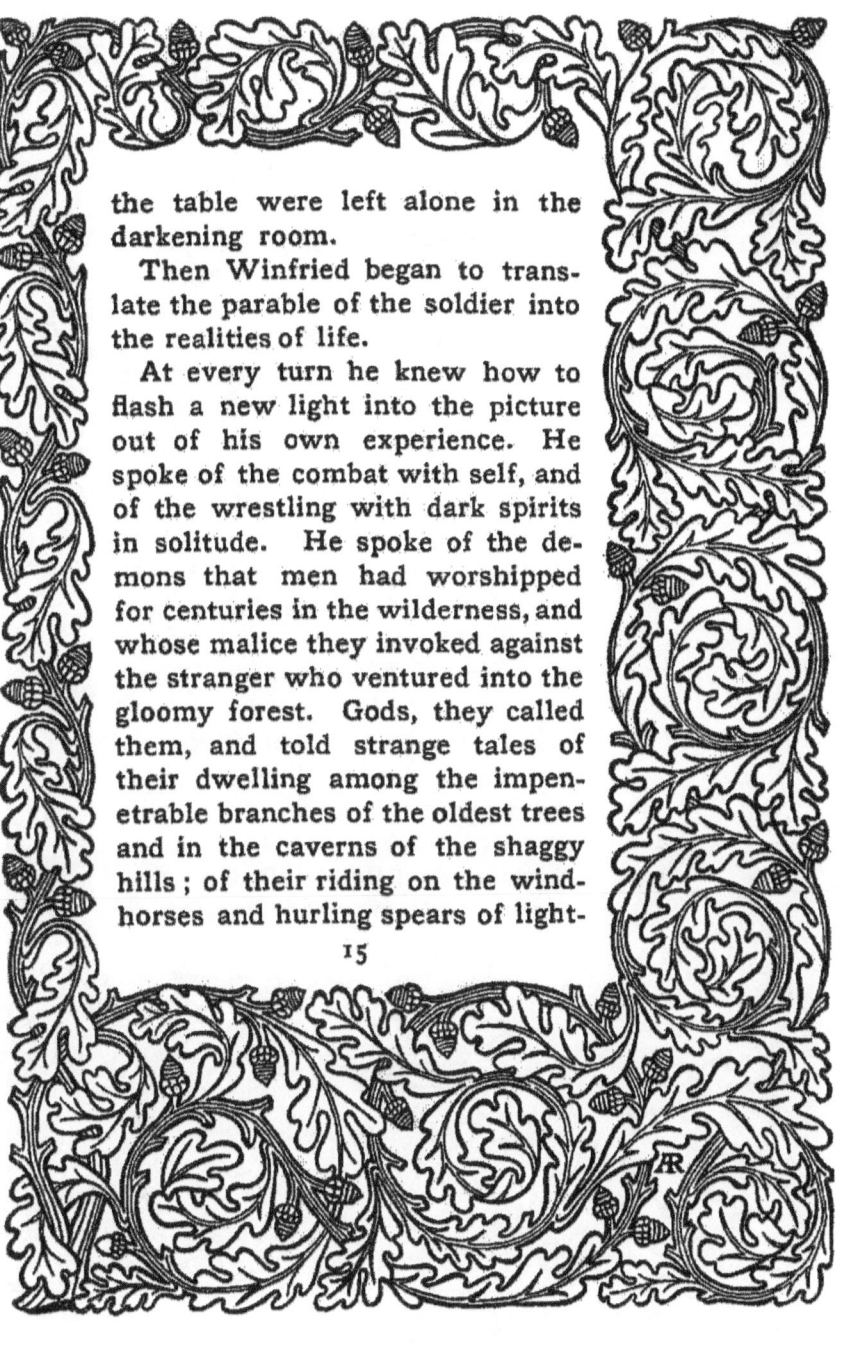

the table were left alone in the darkening room.

Then Winfried began to translate the parable of the soldier into the realities of life.

At every turn he knew how to flash a new light into the picture out of his own experience. He spoke of the combat with self, and of the wrestling with dark spirits in solitude. He spoke of the demons that men had worshipped for centuries in the wilderness, and whose malice they invoked against the stranger who ventured into the gloomy forest. Gods, they called them, and told strange tales of their dwelling among the impenetrable branches of the oldest trees and in the caverns of the shaggy hills; of their riding on the wind-horses and hurling spears of light-

15

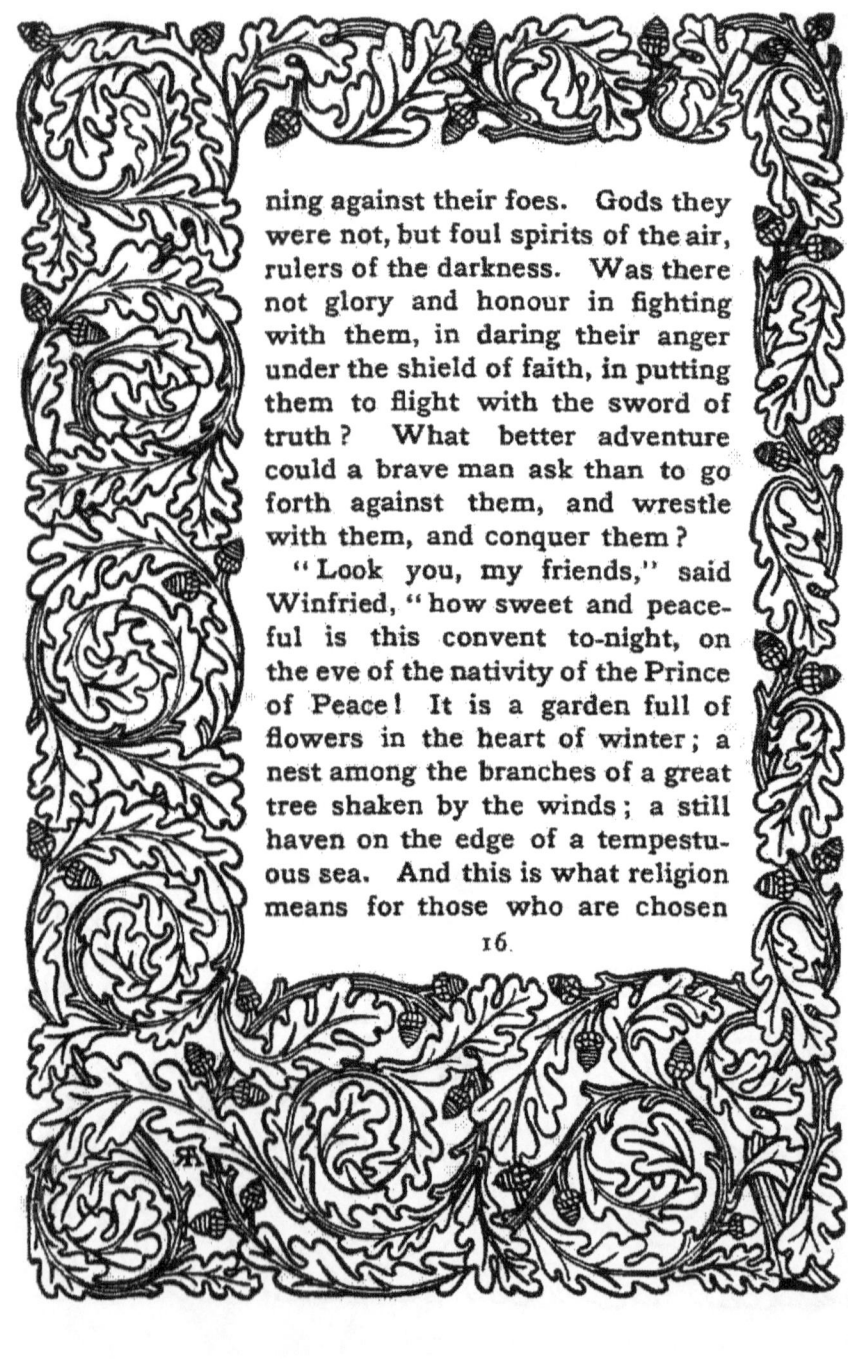

ning against their foes. Gods they
were not, but foul spirits of the air,
rulers of the darkness. Was there
not glory and honour in fighting
with them, in daring their anger
under the shield of faith, in putting
them to flight with the sword of
truth? What better adventure
could a brave man ask than to go
forth against them, and wrestle
with them, and conquer them?

"Look you, my friends," said
Winfried, "how sweet and peaceful is this convent to-night, on
the eve of the nativity of the Prince
of Peace! It is a garden full of
flowers in the heart of winter; a
nest among the branches of a great
tree shaken by the winds; a still
haven on the edge of a tempestu-
ous sea. And this is what religion
means for those who are chosen

16.

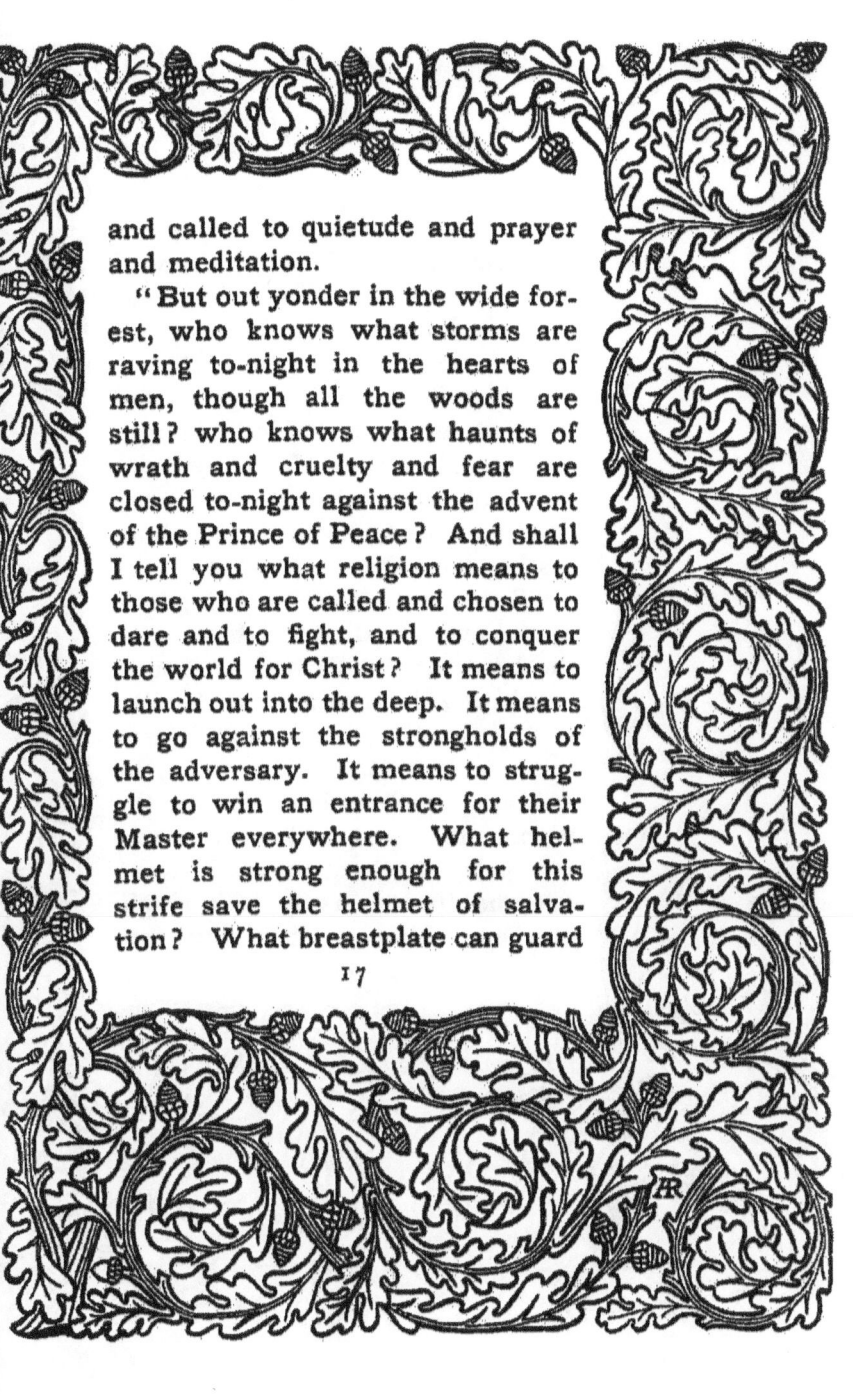

and called to quietude and prayer and meditation.

"But out yonder in the wide forest, who knows what storms are raving to-night in the hearts of men, though all the woods are still? who knows what haunts of wrath and cruelty and fear are closed to-night against the advent of the Prince of Peace? And shall I tell you what religion means to those who are called and chosen to dare and to fight, and to conquer the world for Christ? It means to launch out into the deep. It means to go against the strongholds of the adversary. It means to struggle to win an entrance for their Master everywhere. What helmet is strong enough for this strife save the helmet of salvation? What breastplate can guard

17

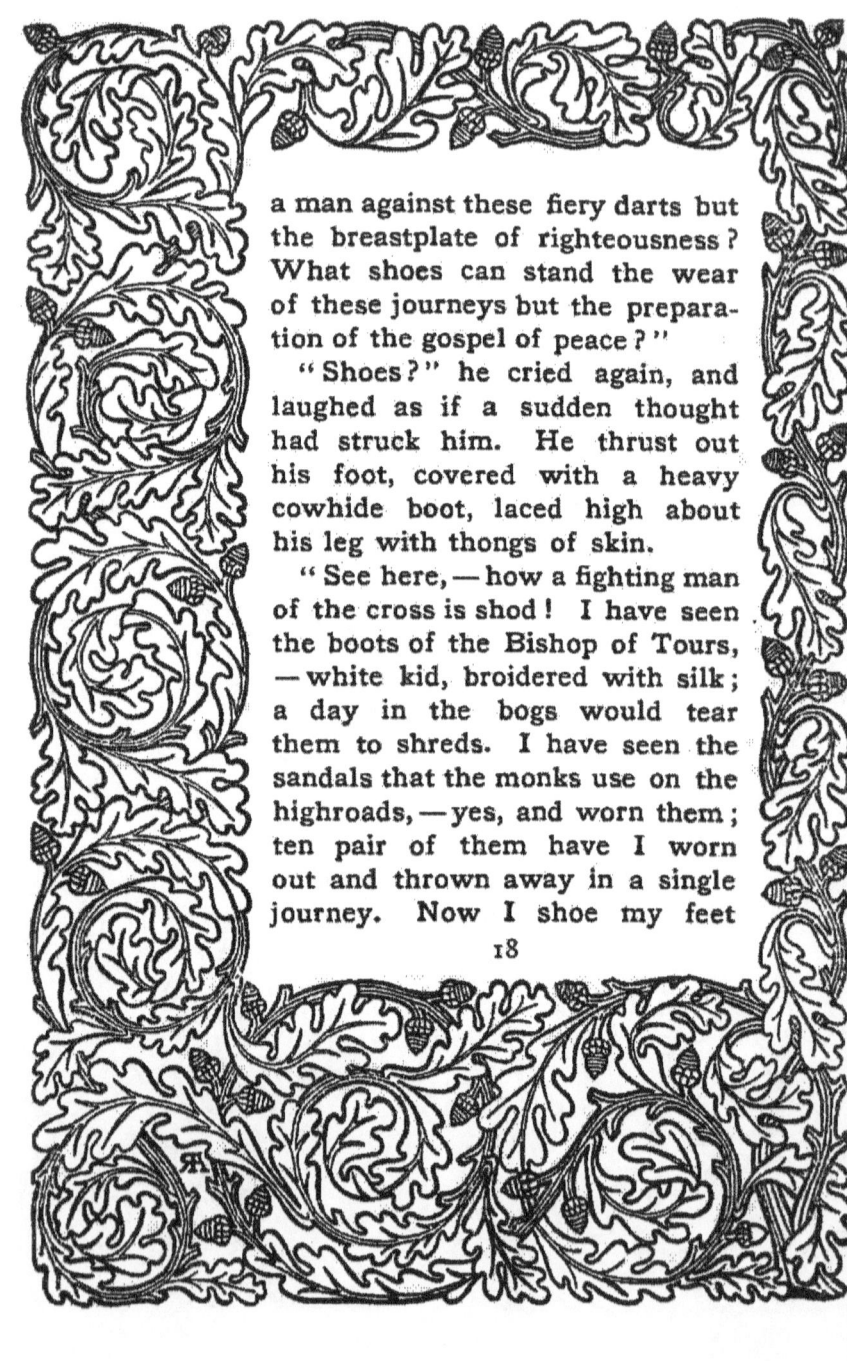

a man against these fiery darts but
the breastplate of righteousness?
What shoes can stand the wear
of these journeys but the preparation of the gospel of peace?"

"Shoes?" he cried again, and
laughed as if a sudden thought
had struck him. He thrust out
his foot, covered with a heavy
cowhide boot, laced high about
his leg with thongs of skin.

"See here,—how a fighting man
of the cross is shod! I have seen
the boots of the Bishop of Tours,
— white kid, broidered with silk;
a day in the bogs would tear
them to shreds. I have seen the
sandals that the monks use on the
highroads,—yes, and worn them;
ten pair of them have I worn
out and thrown away in a single
journey. Now I shoe my feet

18

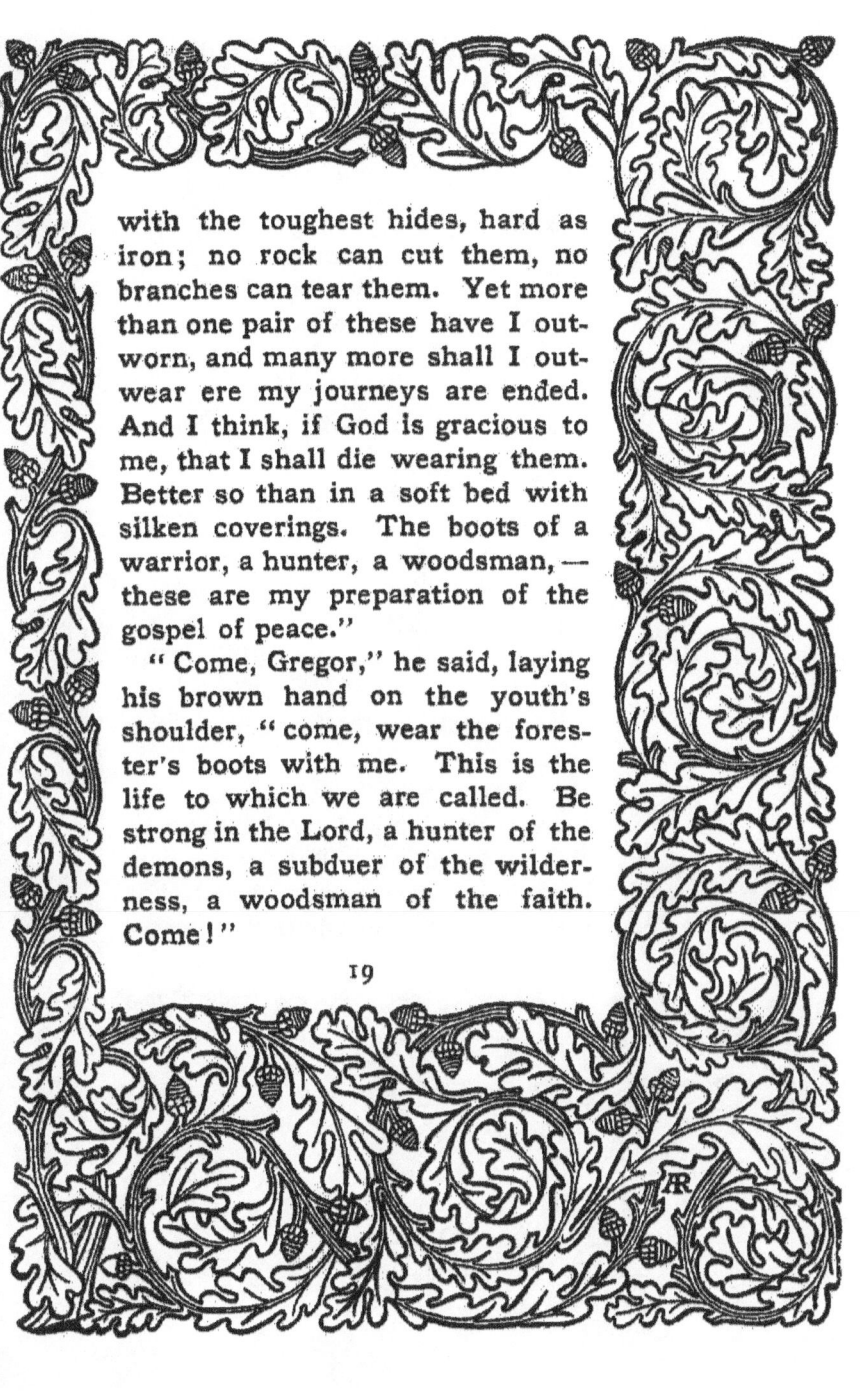

with the toughest hides, hard as iron; no rock can cut them, no branches can tear them. Yet more than one pair of these have I outworn, and many more shall I outwear ere my journeys are ended. And I think, if God is gracious to me, that I shall die wearing them. Better so than in a soft bed with silken coverings. The boots of a warrior, a hunter, a woodsman, — these are my preparation of the gospel of peace."

"Come, Gregor," he said, laying his brown hand on the youth's shoulder, "come, wear the forester's boots with me. This is the life to which we are called. Be strong in the Lord, a hunter of the demons, a subduer of the wilderness, a woodsman of the faith. Come!"

19

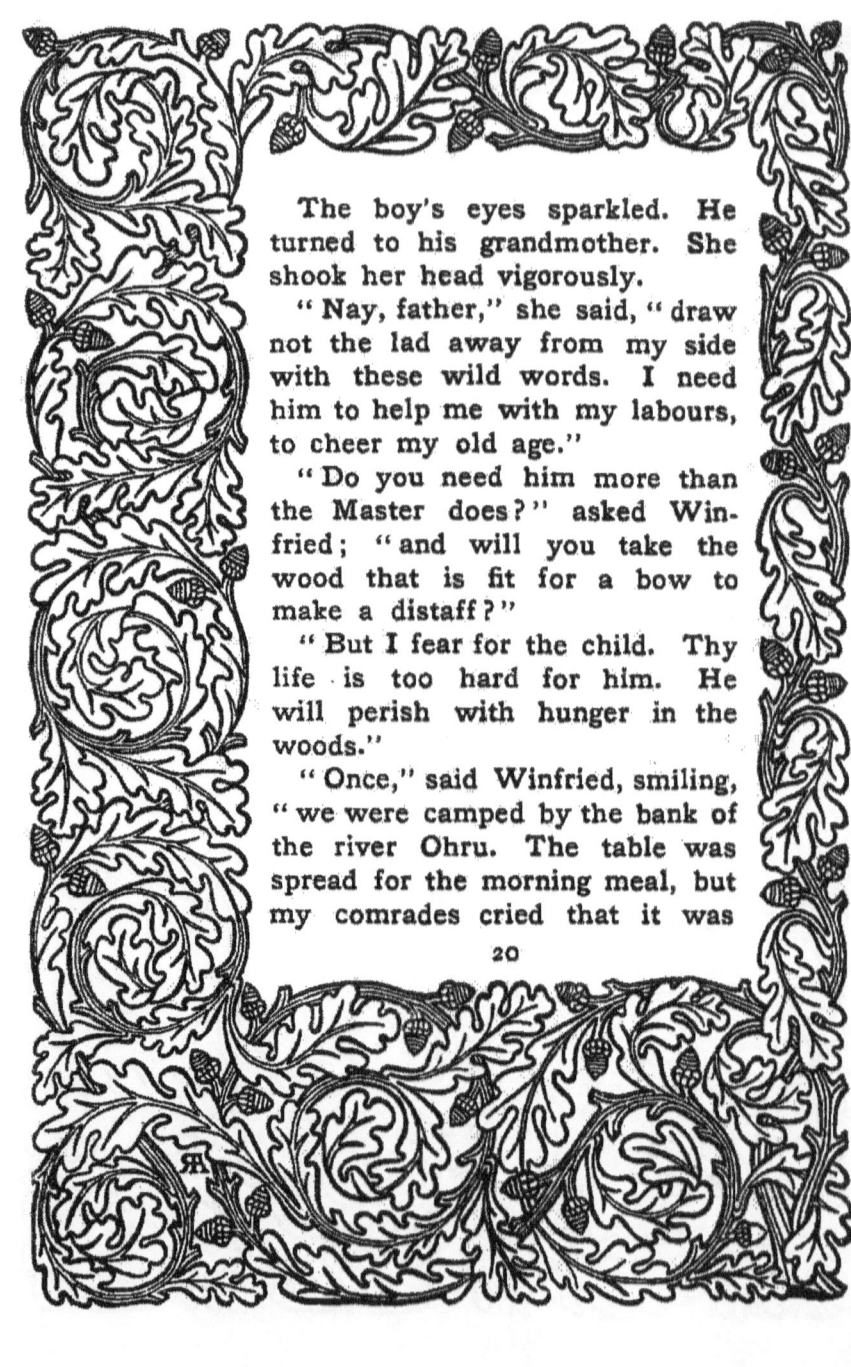

The boy's eyes sparkled. He turned to his grandmother. She shook her head vigorously.

"Nay, father," she said, "draw not the lad away from my side with these wild words. I need him to help me with my labours, to cheer my old age."

"Do you need him more than the Master does?" asked Winfried; "and will you take the wood that is fit for a bow to make a distaff?"

"But I fear for the child. Thy life is too hard for him. He will perish with hunger in the woods."

"Once," said Winfried, smiling, "we were camped by the bank of the river Ohru. The table was spread for the morning meal, but my comrades cried that it was

20

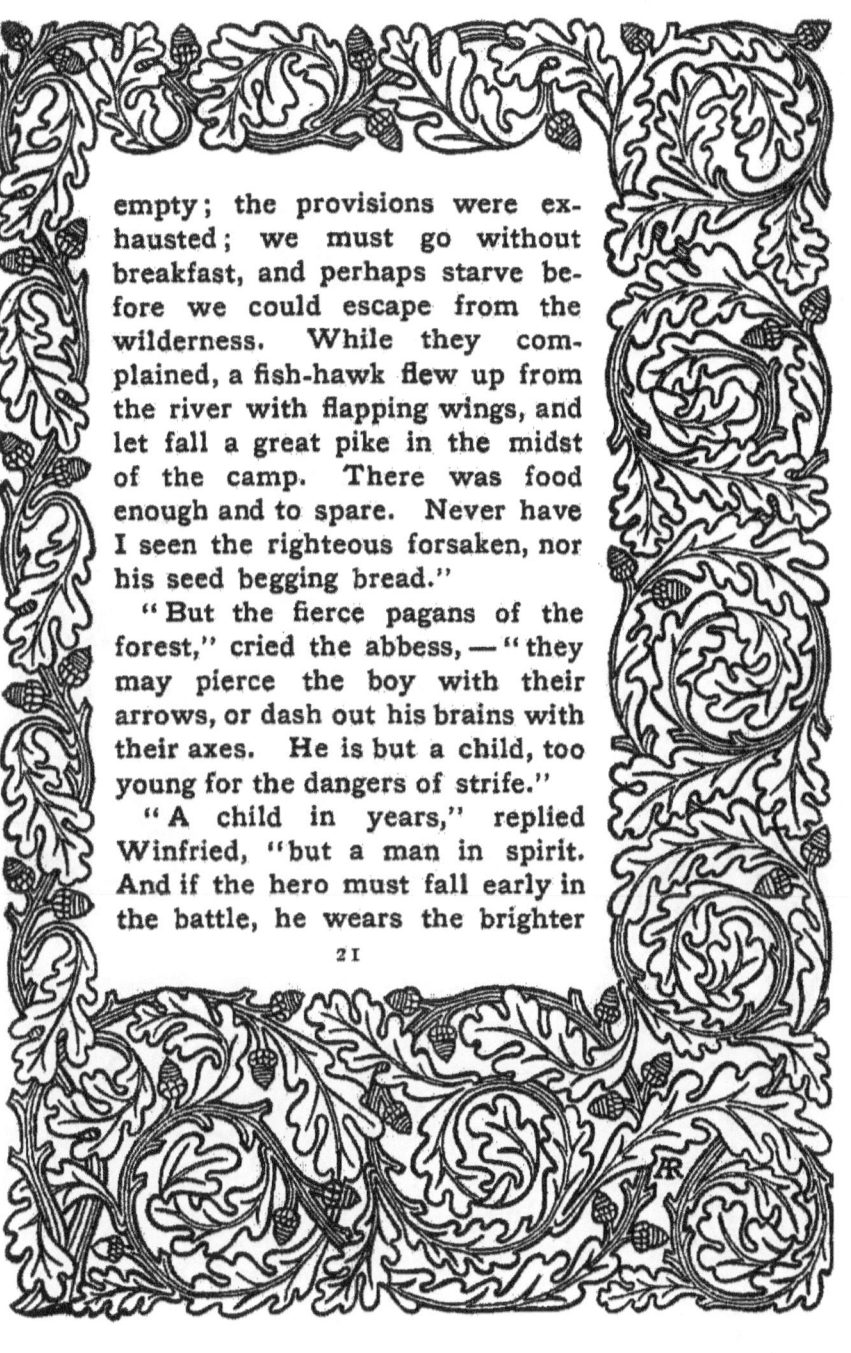

empty; the provisions were exhausted; we must go without breakfast, and perhaps starve before we could escape from the wilderness. While they complained, a fish-hawk flew up from the river with flapping wings, and let fall a great pike in the midst of the camp. There was food enough and to spare. Never have I seen the righteous forsaken, nor his seed begging bread."

"But the fierce pagans of the forest," cried the abbess, — "they may pierce the boy with their arrows, or dash out his brains with their axes. He is but a child, too young for the dangers of strife."

"A child in years," replied Winfried, "but a man in spirit. And if the hero must fall early in the battle, he wears the brighter

21

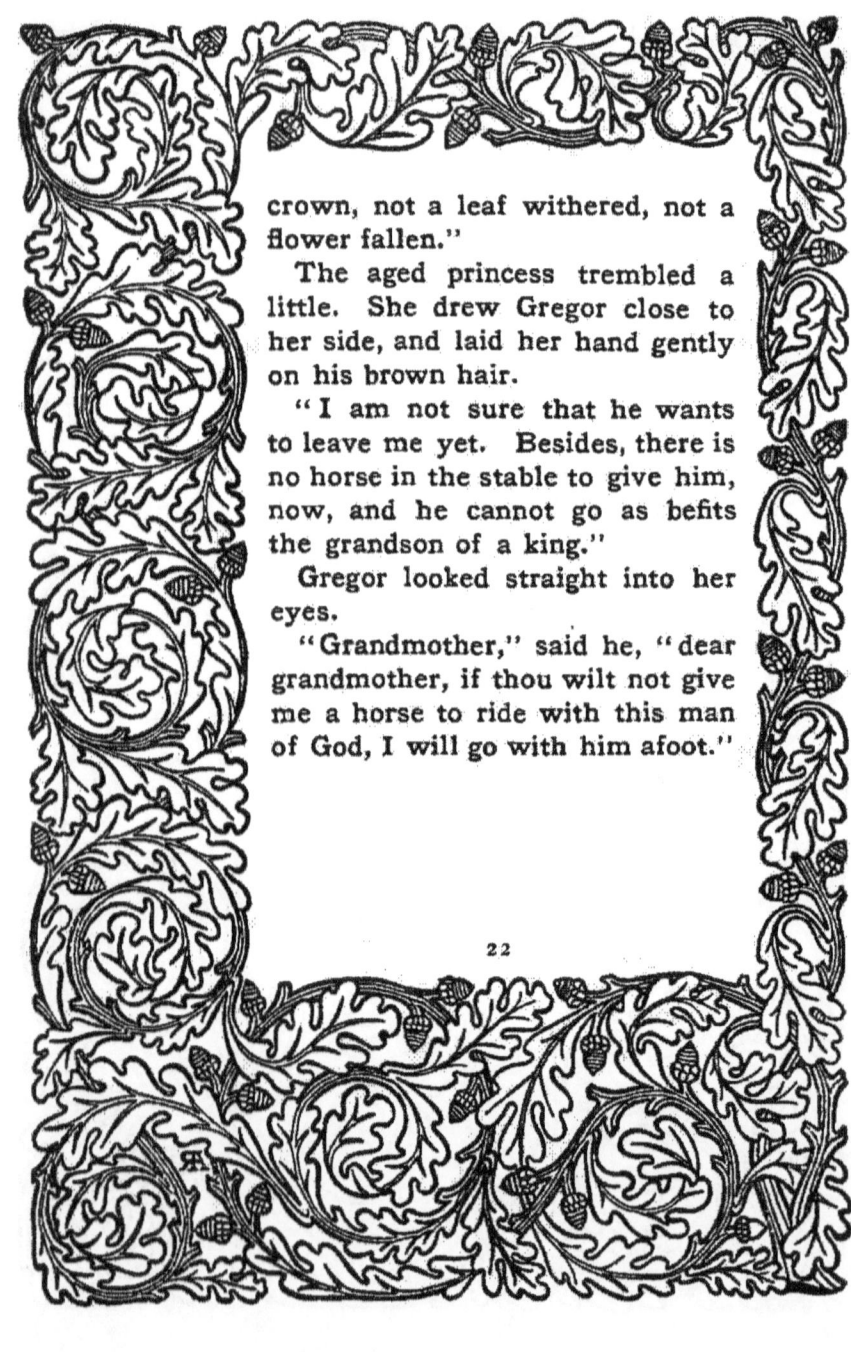

crown, not a leaf withered, not a flower fallen."

The aged princess trembled a little. She drew Gregor close to her side, and laid her hand gently on his brown hair.

"I am not sure that he wants to leave me yet. Besides, there is no horse in the stable to give him, now, and he cannot go as befits the grandson of a king."

Gregor looked straight into her eyes.

"Grandmother," said he, "dear grandmother, if thou wilt not give me a horse to ride with this man of God, I will go with him afoot."

22

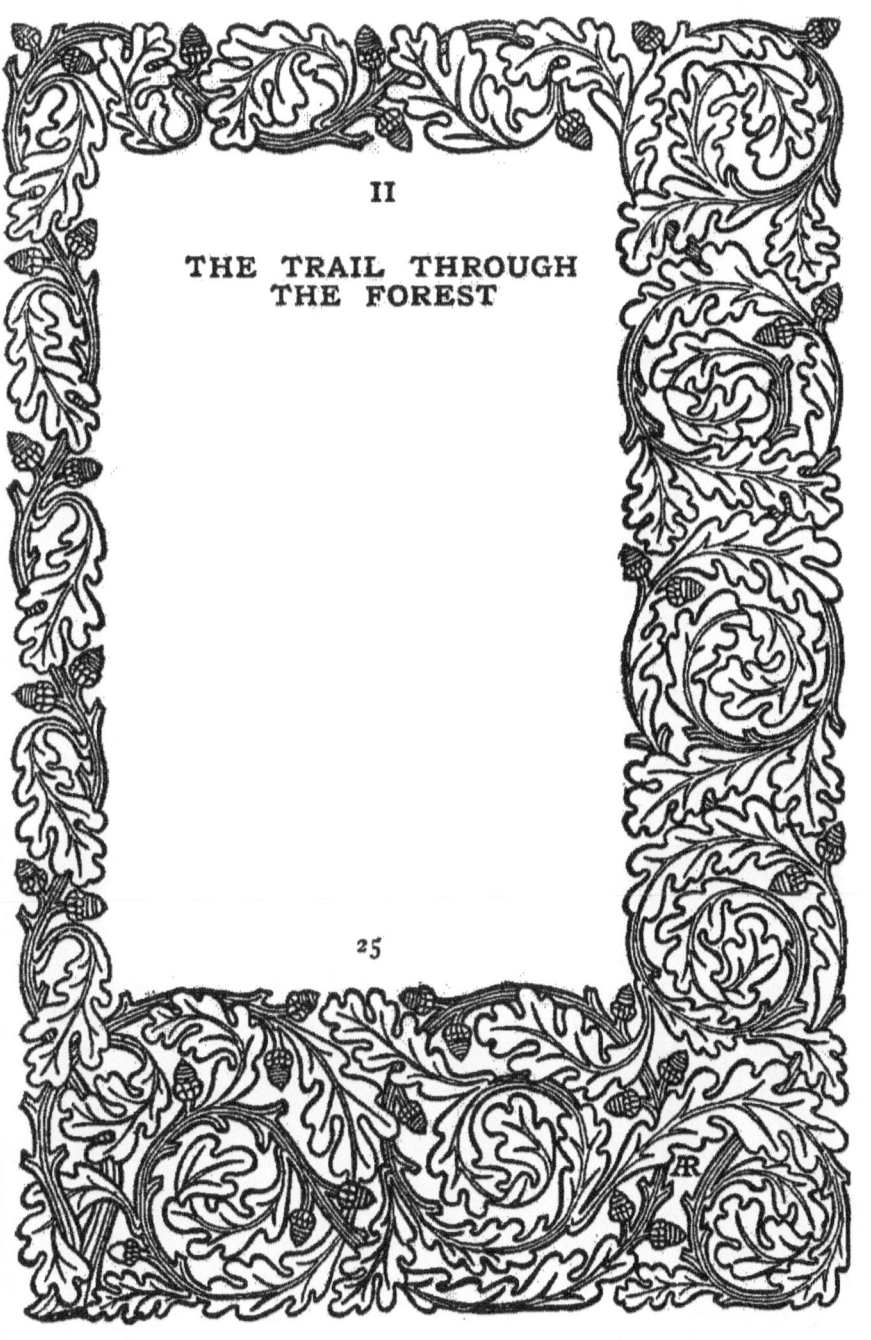

II

THE TRAIL THROUGH THE FOREST

25

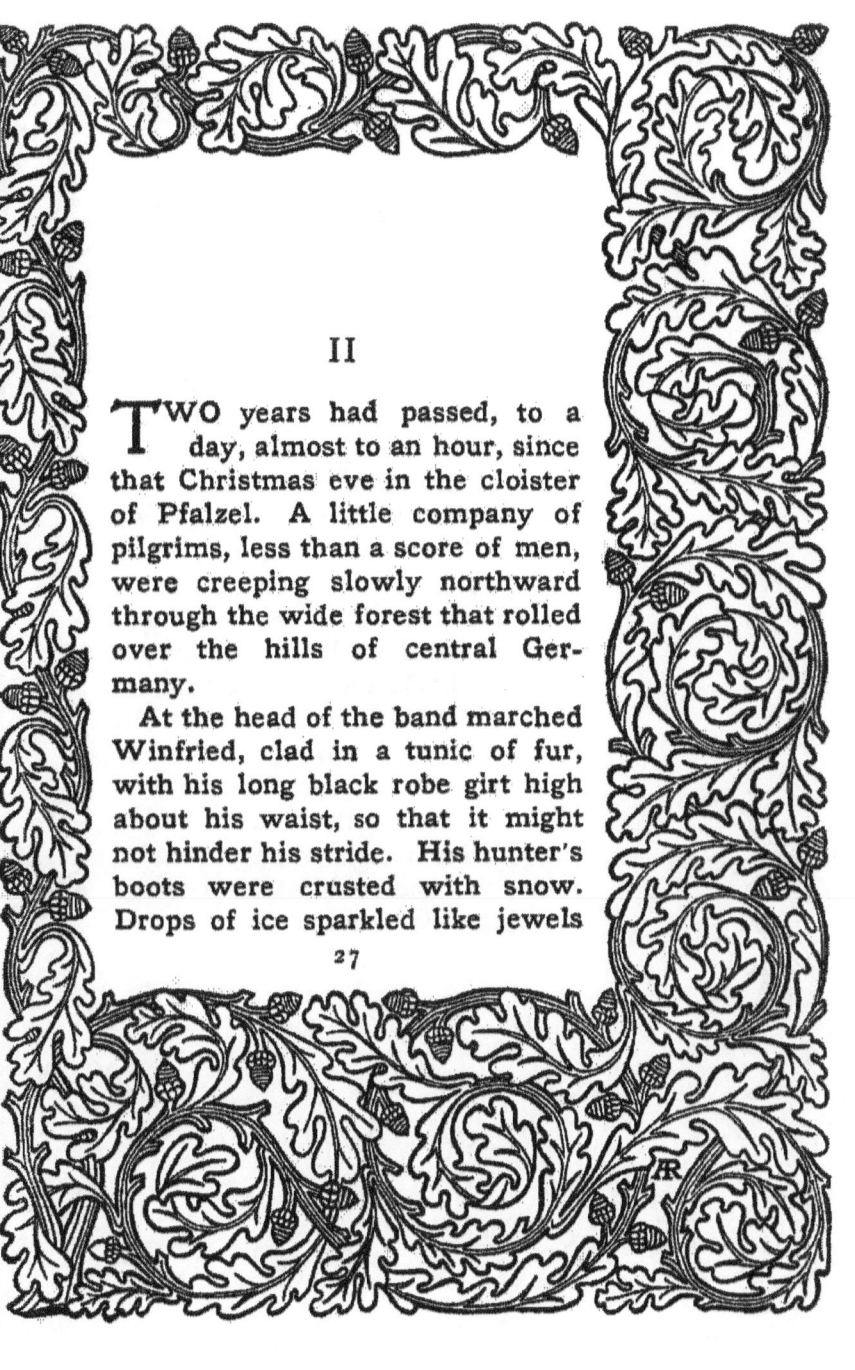

II

TWO years had passed, to a day, almost to an hour, since that Christmas eve in the cloister of Pfalzel. A little company of pilgrims, less than a score of men, were creeping slowly northward through the wide forest that rolled over the hills of central Germany.

At the head of the band marched Winfried, clad in a tunic of fur, with his long black robe girt high about his waist, so that it might not hinder his stride. His hunter's boots were crusted with snow. Drops of ice sparkled like jewels

27

along the thongs that bound his legs. There was no other ornament to his dress except the bishop's cross hanging on his breast, and the broad silver clasp that fastened his cloak about his neck. He carried a strong, tall staff in his hand, fashioned at the top into the form of a cross.

Close beside him, keeping step like a familiar comrade, was the young Prince Gregor. Long marches through the wilderness had stretched his limbs and broadened his back, and made a man of him in stature as well as in spirit. His jacket and cap were of wolf-skin, and on his shoulder he carried an axe, with broad, shining blade. He was a mighty woodsman now, and could make a spray of chips fly around him as he

28

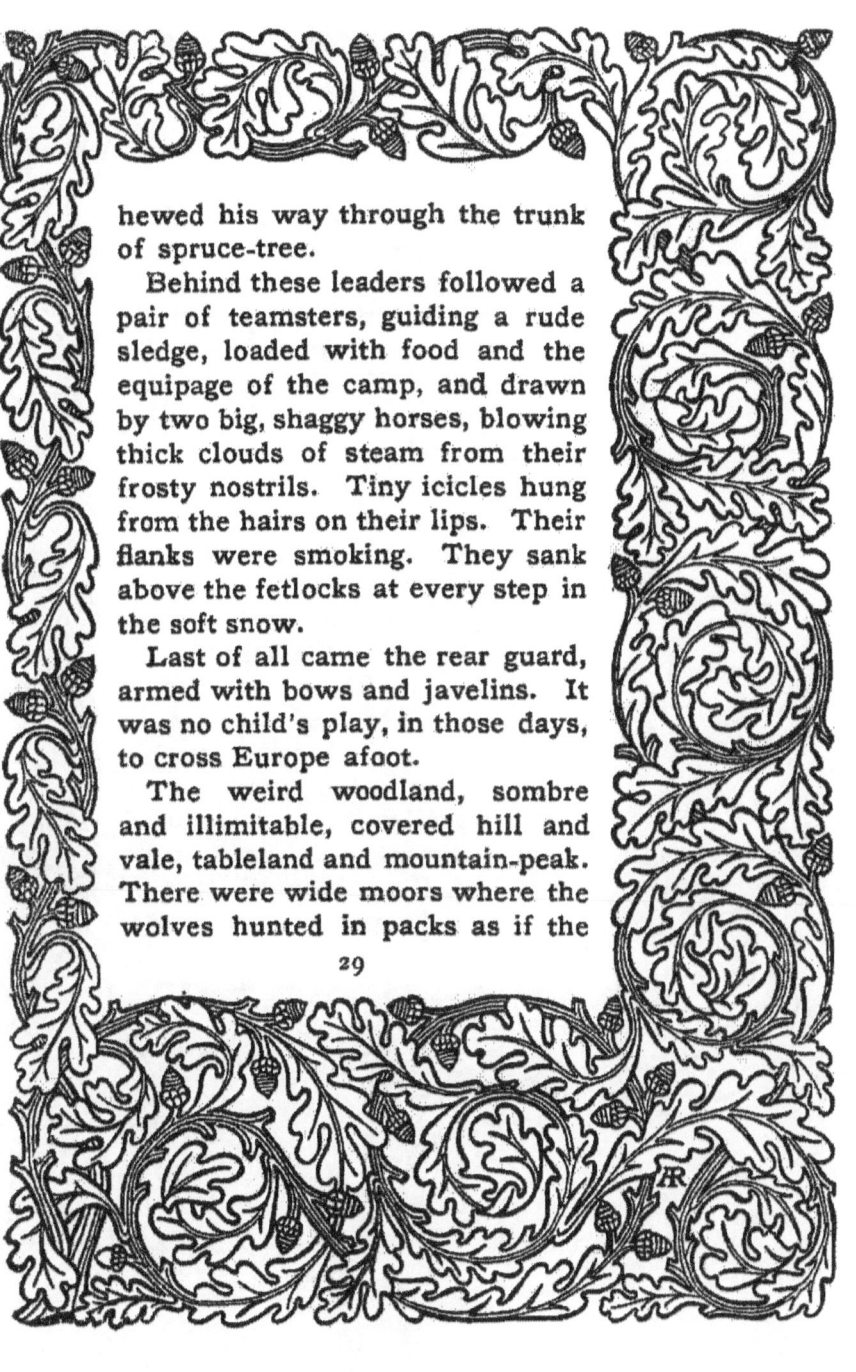

hewed his way through the trunk
of spruce-tree.

Behind these leaders followed a
pair of teamsters, guiding a rude
sledge, loaded with food and the
equipage of the camp, and drawn
by two big, shaggy horses, blowing
thick clouds of steam from their
frosty nostrils. Tiny icicles hung
from the hairs on their lips. Their
flanks were smoking. They sank
above the fetlocks at every step in
the soft snow.

Last of all came the rear guard,
armed with bows and javelins. It
was no child's play, in those days,
to cross Europe afoot.

The weird woodland, sombre
and illimitable, covered hill and
vale, tableland and mountain-peak.
There were wide moors where the
wolves hunted in packs as if the

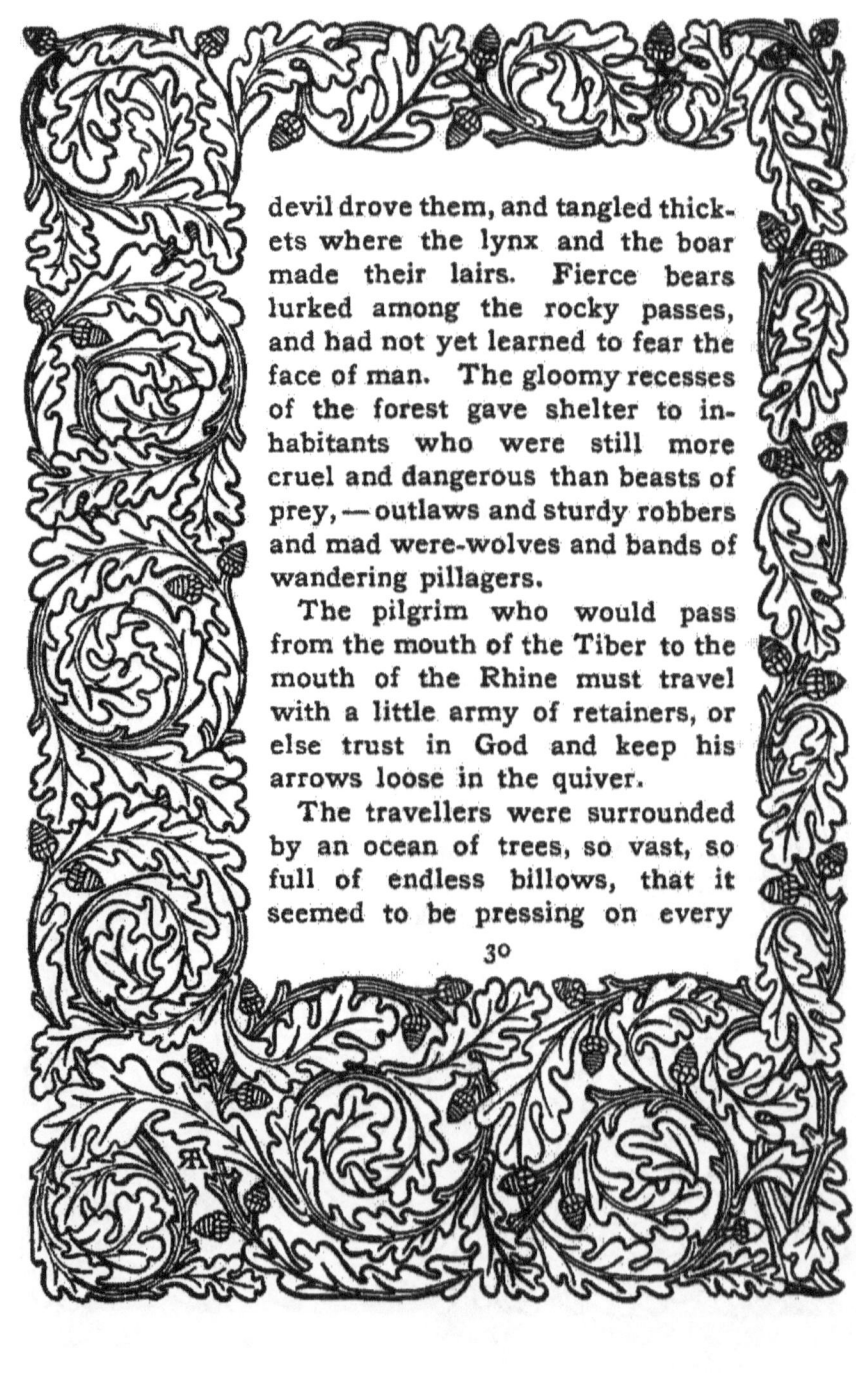

devil drove them, and tangled thick-
ets where the lynx and the boar
made their lairs. Fierce bears
lurked among the rocky passes,
and had not yet learned to fear the
face of man. The gloomy recesses
of the forest gave shelter to in-
habitants who were still more
cruel and dangerous than beasts of
prey, — outlaws and sturdy robbers
and mad were-wolves and bands of
wandering pillagers.

The pilgrim who would pass
from the mouth of the Tiber to the
mouth of the Rhine must travel
with a little army of retainers, or
else trust in God and keep his
arrows loose in the quiver.

The travellers were surrounded
by an ocean of trees, so vast, so
full of endless billows, that it
seemed to be pressing on every

30

side to overwhelm them. Gnarled
oaks, with branches twisted and
knotted as if in rage, rose in groves
like tidal waves. Smooth forests
of beech-trees, round and gray,
swept over the knolls and slopes
of land in a mighty ground-swell.
But most of all, the multitude of
pines and firs, innumerable and
monotonous, with straight, stark
trunks, and branches woven together in an unbroken flood of
darkest green, crowded through
the valleys and over the hills,
rising on the highest ridges into
ragged crests, like the foaming
edge of breakers.

Through this sea of shadows ran
a narrow stream of shining white-
ness, — an ancient Roman road,
covered with snow. It was as if
some great ship had ploughed

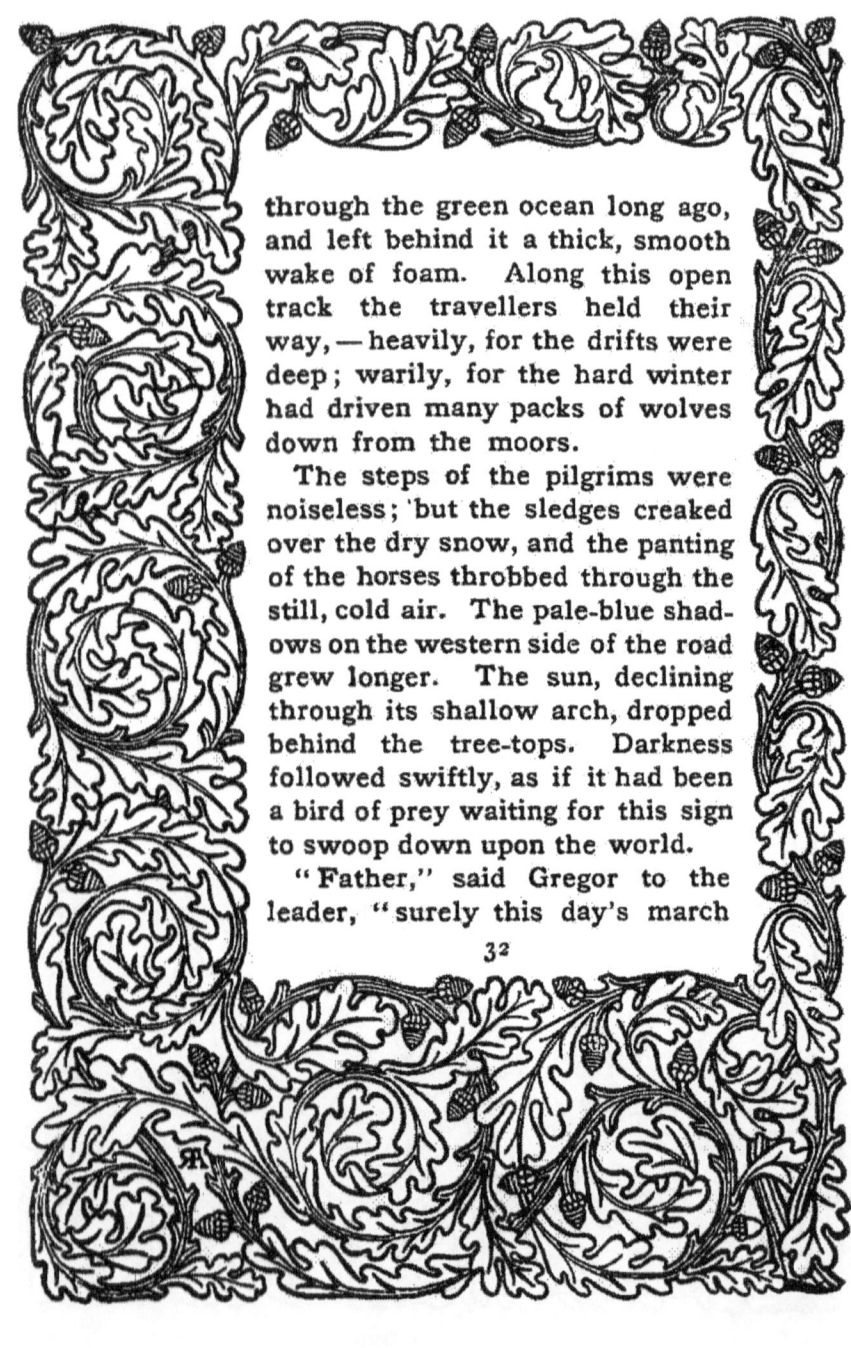

through the green ocean long ago, and left behind it a thick, smooth wake of foam. Along this open track the travellers held their way,—heavily, for the drifts were deep; warily, for the hard winter had driven many packs of wolves down from the moors.

The steps of the pilgrims were noiseless; but the sledges creaked over the dry snow, and the panting of the horses throbbed through the still, cold air. The pale-blue shadows on the western side of the road grew longer. The sun, declining through its shallow arch, dropped behind the tree-tops. Darkness followed swiftly, as if it had been a bird of prey waiting for this sign to swoop down upon the world.

"Father," said Gregor to the leader, "surely this day's march

32

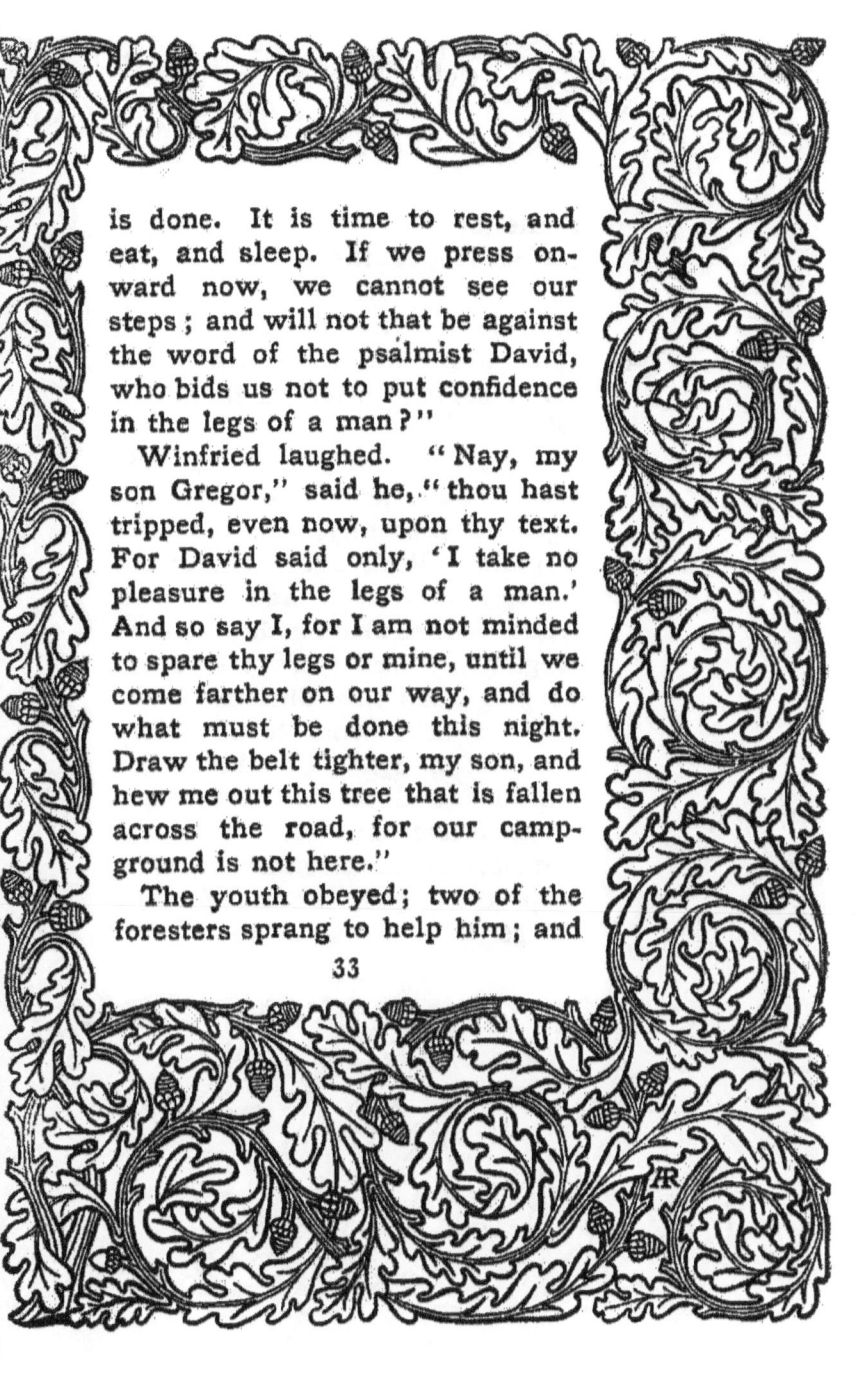

is done. It is time to rest, and eat, and sleep. If we press onward now, we cannot see our steps; and will not that be against the word of the psalmist David, who bids us not to put confidence in the legs of a man?"

Winfried laughed. "Nay, my son Gregor," said he, "thou hast tripped, even now, upon thy text. For David said only, 'I take no pleasure in the legs of a man.' And so say I, for I am not minded to spare thy legs or mine, until we come farther on our way, and do what must be done this night. Draw the belt tighter, my son, and hew me out this tree that is fallen across the road, for our campground is not here."

The youth obeyed; two of the foresters sprang to help him; and

33

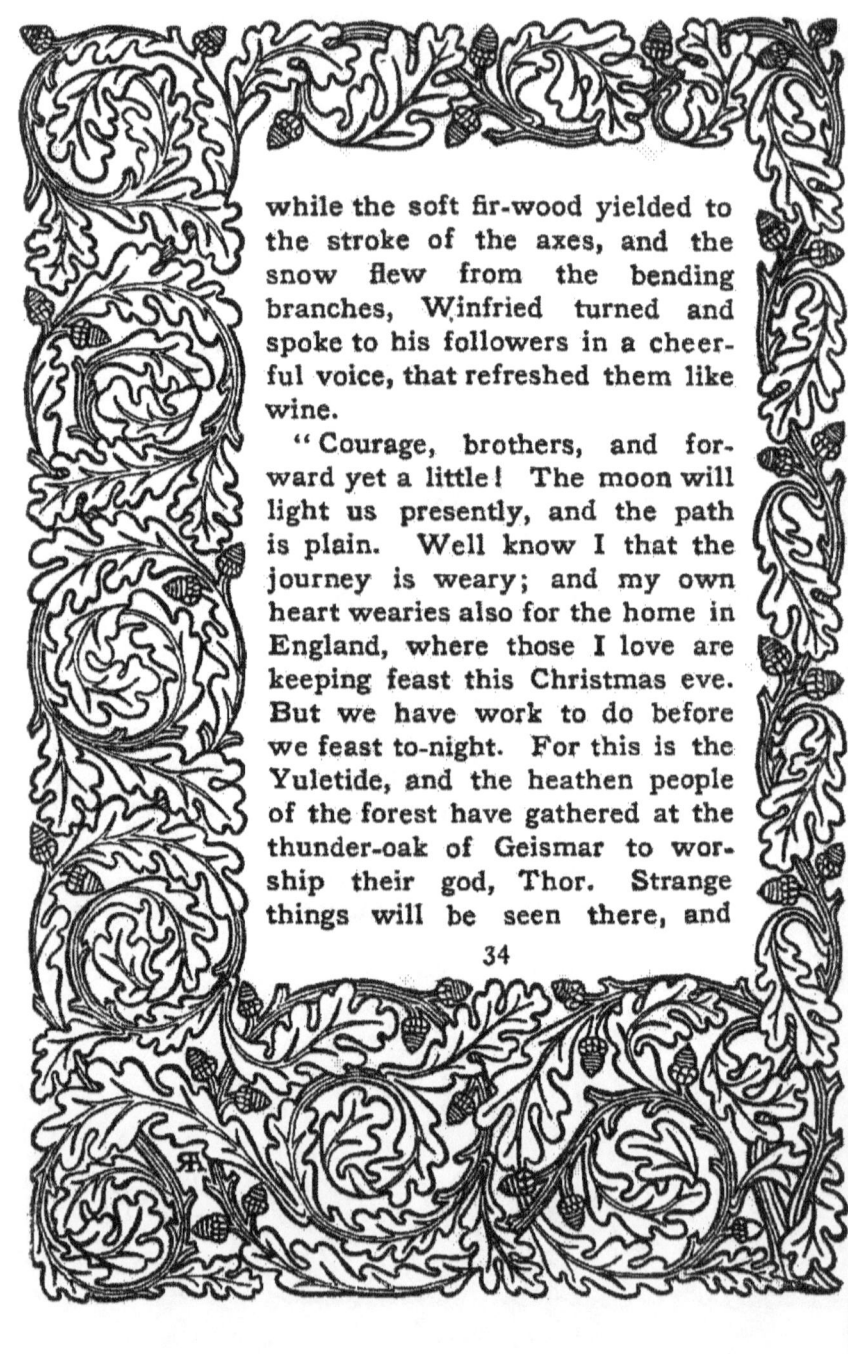

while the soft fir-wood yielded to the stroke of the axes, and the snow flew from the bending branches, Winfried turned and spoke to his followers in a cheerful voice, that refreshed them like wine.

"Courage, brothers, and forward yet a little! The moon will light us presently, and the path is plain. Well know I that the journey is weary; and my own heart wearies also for the home in England, where those I love are keeping feast this Christmas eve. But we have work to do before we feast to-night. For this is the Yuletide, and the heathen people of the forest have gathered at the thunder-oak of Geismar to worship their god, Thor. Strange things will be seen there, and

34

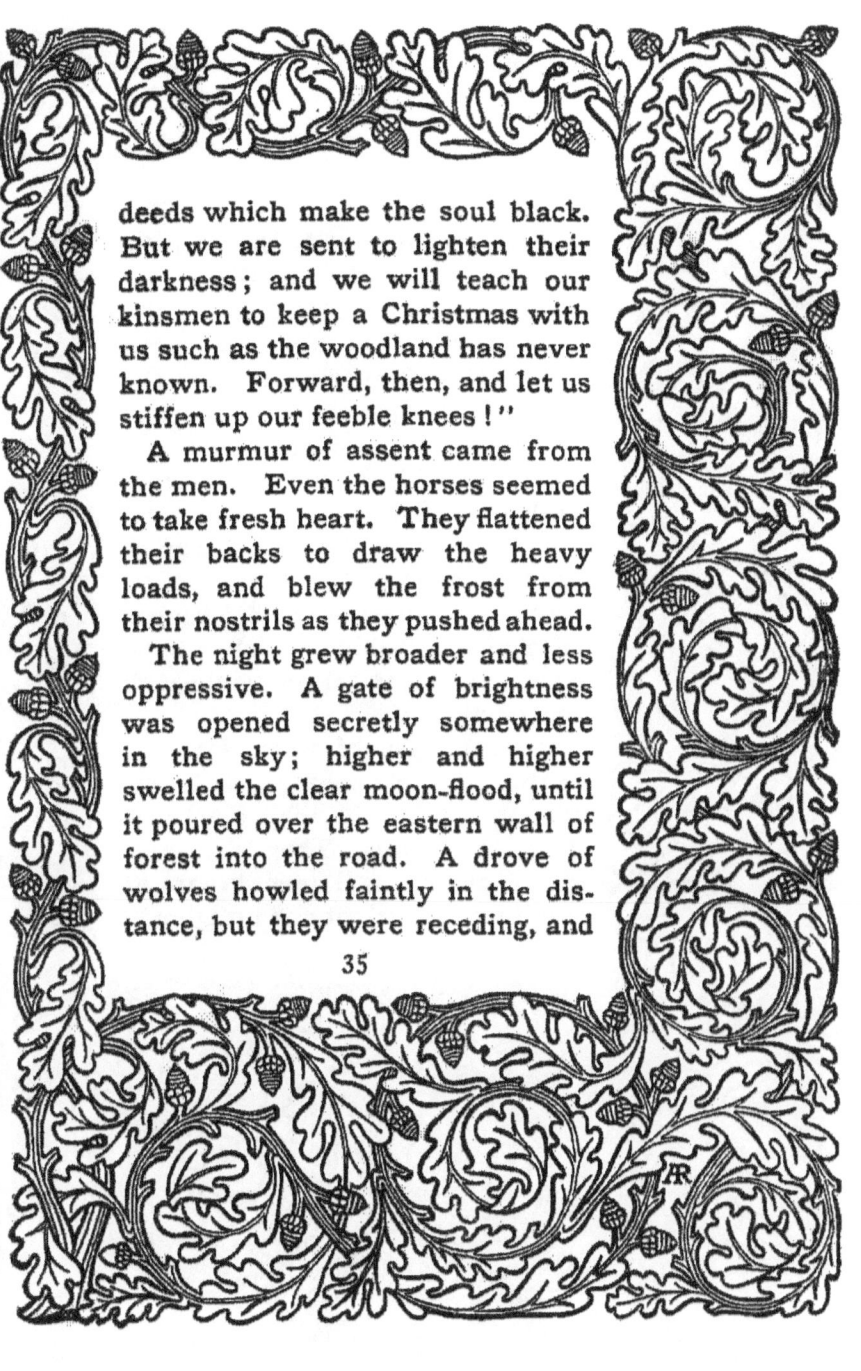

deeds which make the soul black. But we are sent to lighten their darkness; and we will teach our kinsmen to keep a Christmas with us such as the woodland has never known. Forward, then, and let us stiffen up our feeble knees!"

A murmur of assent came from the men. Even the horses seemed to take fresh heart. They flattened their backs to draw the heavy loads, and blew the frost from their nostrils as they pushed ahead.

The night grew broader and less oppressive. A gate of brightness was opened secretly somewhere in the sky; higher and higher swelled the clear moon-flood, until it poured over the eastern wall of forest into the road. A drove of wolves howled faintly in the distance, but they were receding, and

35

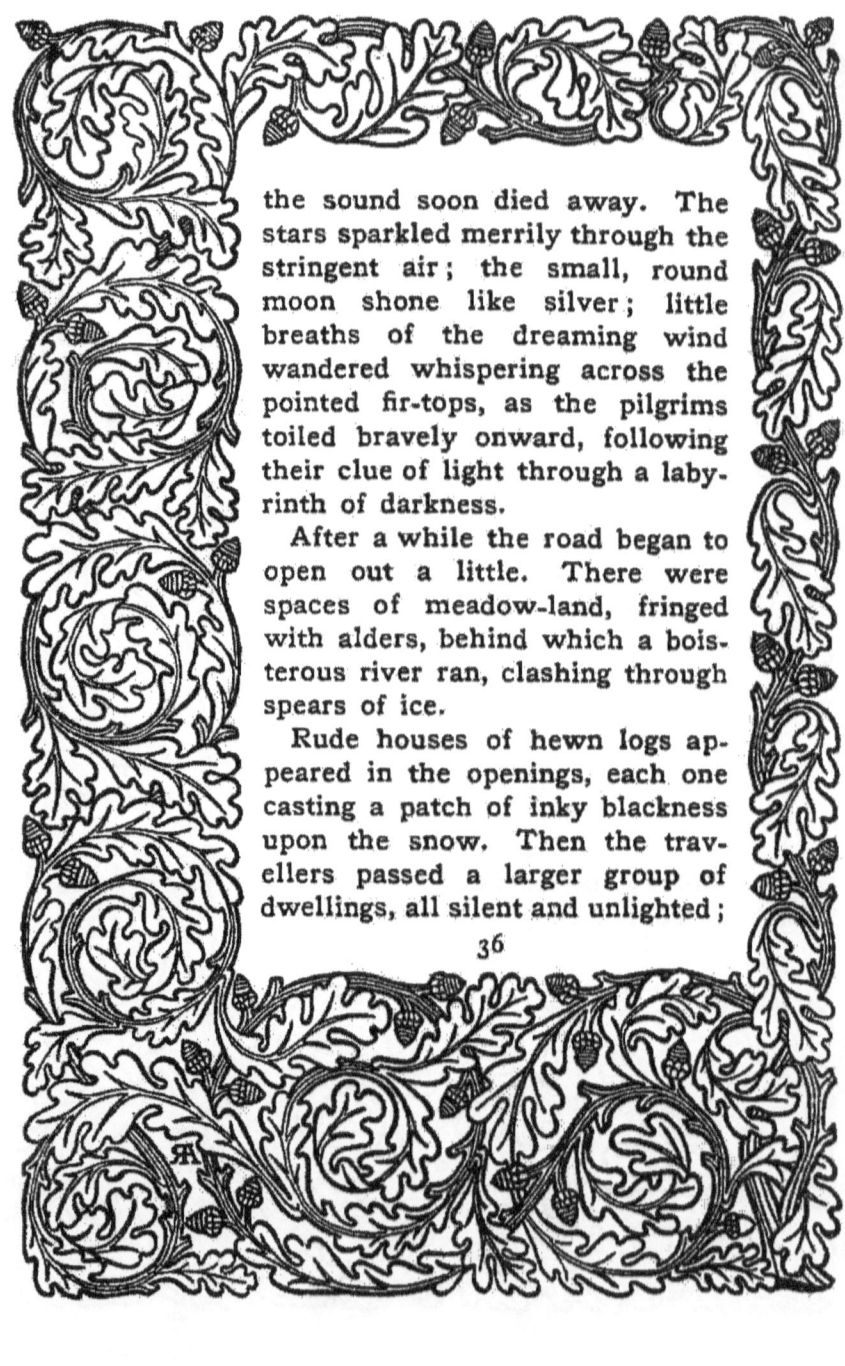

the sound soon died away. The
stars sparkled merrily through the
stringent air; the small, round
moon shone like silver; little
breaths of the dreaming wind
wandered whispering across the
pointed fir-tops, as the pilgrims
toiled bravely onward, following
their clue of light through a laby-
rinth of darkness.

After a while the road began to
open out a little. There were
spaces of meadow-land, fringed
with alders, behind which a bois-
terous river ran, clashing through
spears of ice.

Rude houses of hewn logs ap-
peared in the openings, each one
casting a patch of inky blackness
upon the snow. Then the travellers passed a larger group of
dwellings, all silent and unlighted;

36

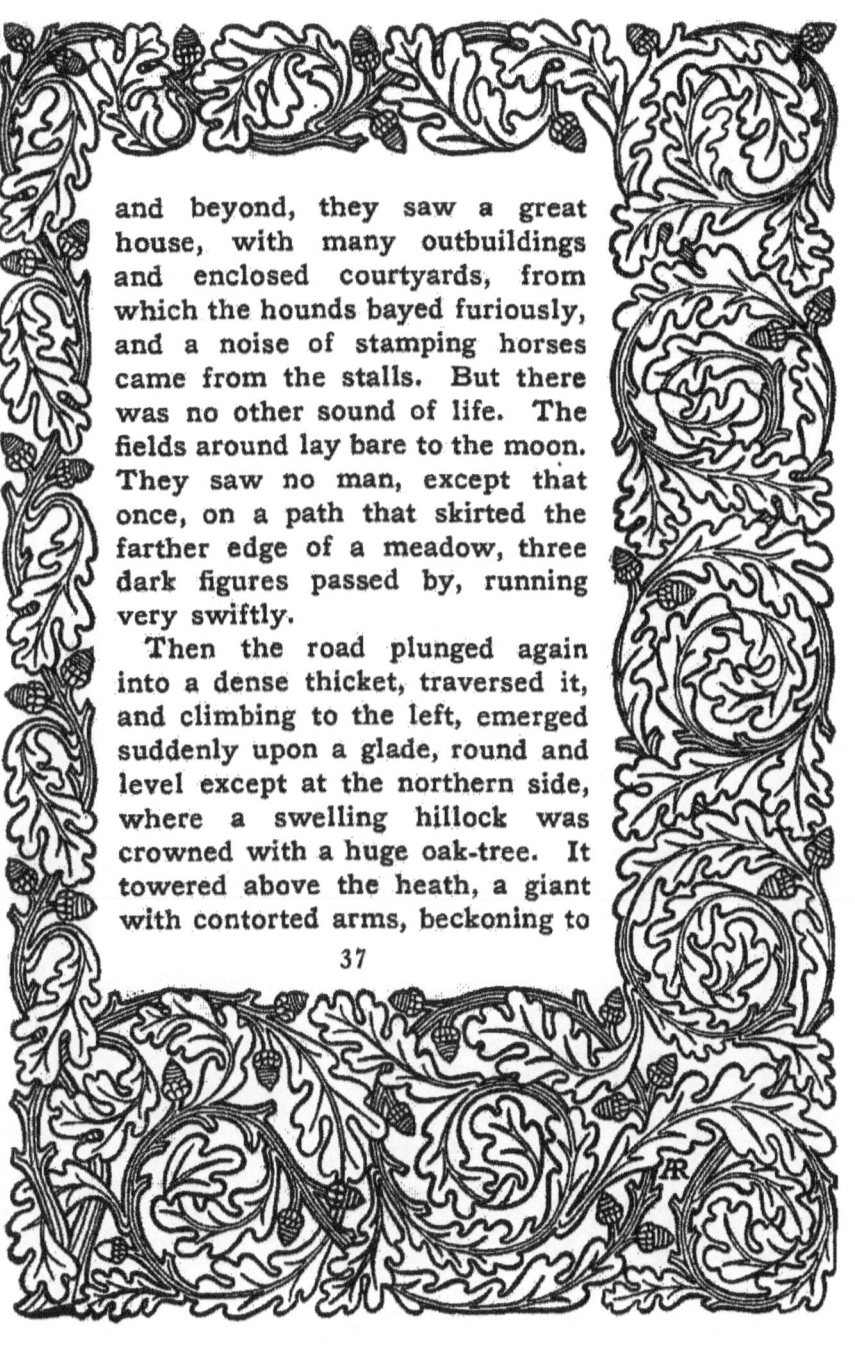

and beyond, they saw a great
house, with many outbuildings
and enclosed courtyards, from
which the hounds bayed furiously,
and a noise of stamping horses
came from the stalls. But there
was no other sound of life. The
fields around lay bare to the moon.
They saw no man, except that
once, on a path that skirted the
farther edge of a meadow, three
dark figures passed by, running
very swiftly.

Then the road plunged again
into a dense thicket, traversed it,
and climbing to the left, emerged
suddenly upon a glade, round and
level except at the northern side,
where a swelling hillock was
crowned with a huge oak-tree. It
towered above the heath, a giant
with contorted arms, beckoning to

37

the host of lesser trees. "Here," cried Winfried, as his eyes flashed and his hand lifted his heavy staff, "here is the Thunder-oak; and here the cross of Christ shall break the hammer of the false god Thor."

38

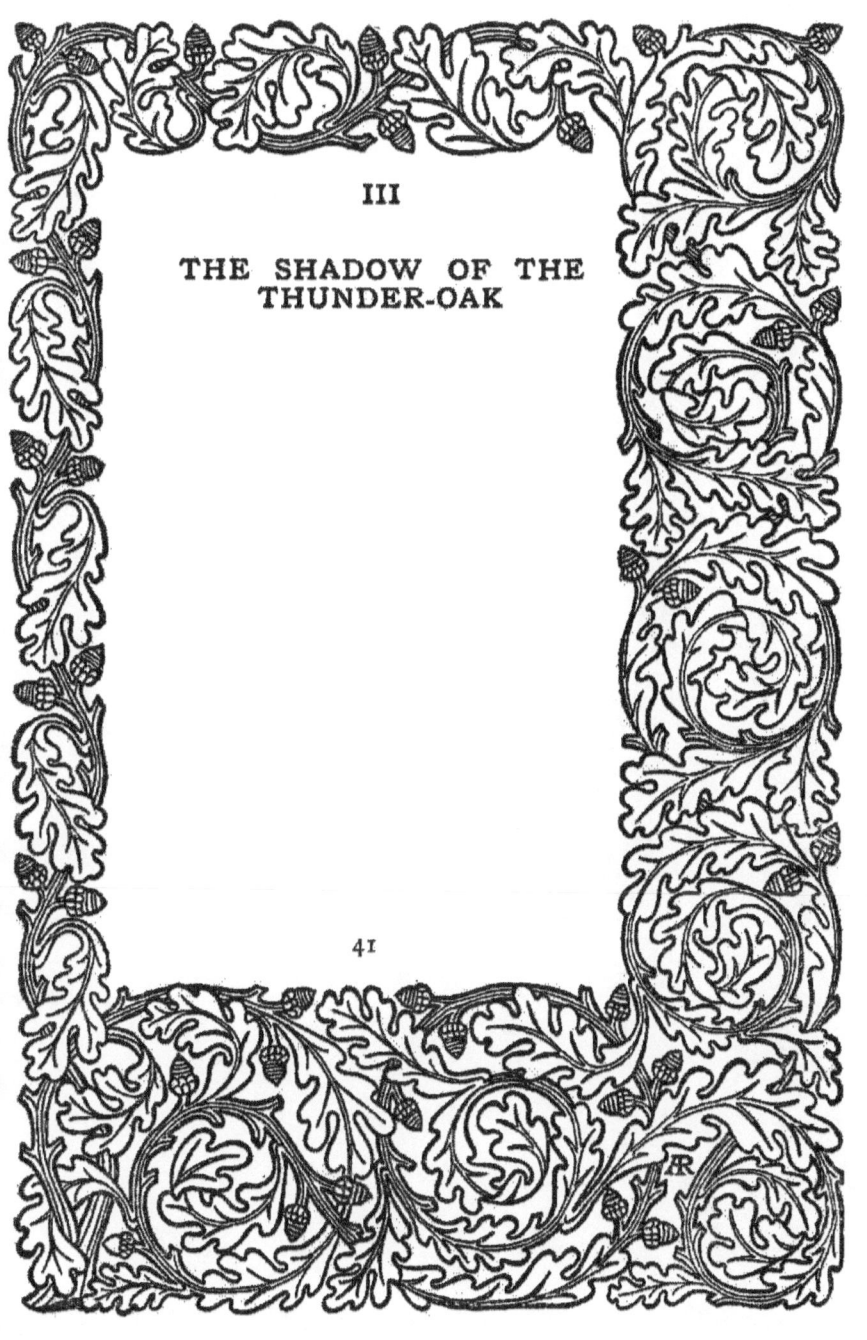

III

THE SHADOW OF THE
THUNDER-OAK

41

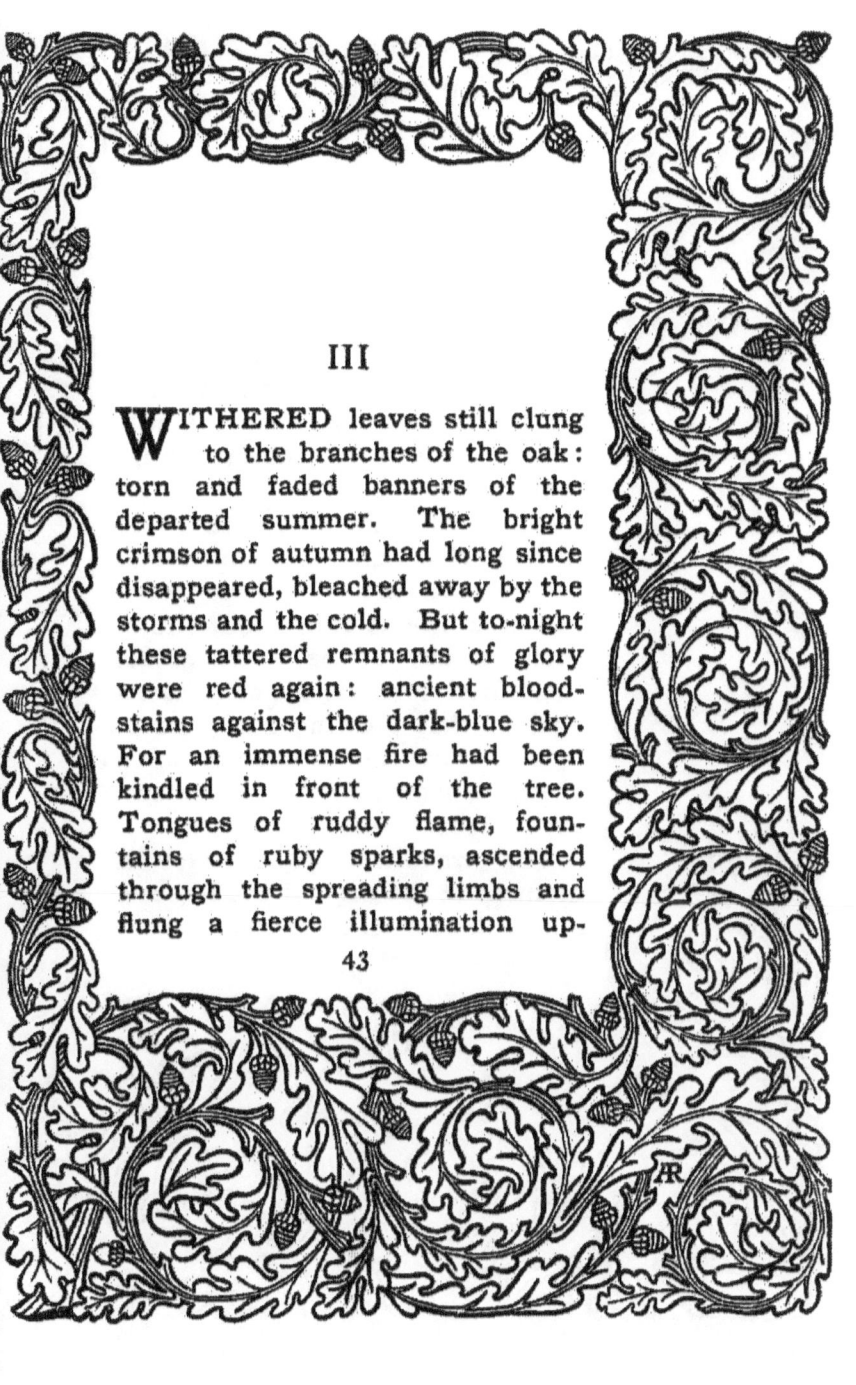

III

WITHERED leaves still clung to the branches of the oak: torn and faded banners of the departed summer. The bright crimson of autumn had long since disappeared, bleached away by the storms and the cold. But to-night these tattered remnants of glory were red again: ancient blood-stains against the dark-blue sky. For an immense fire had been kindled in front of the tree. Tongues of ruddy flame, fountains of ruby sparks, ascended through the spreading limbs and flung a fierce illumination up-

43

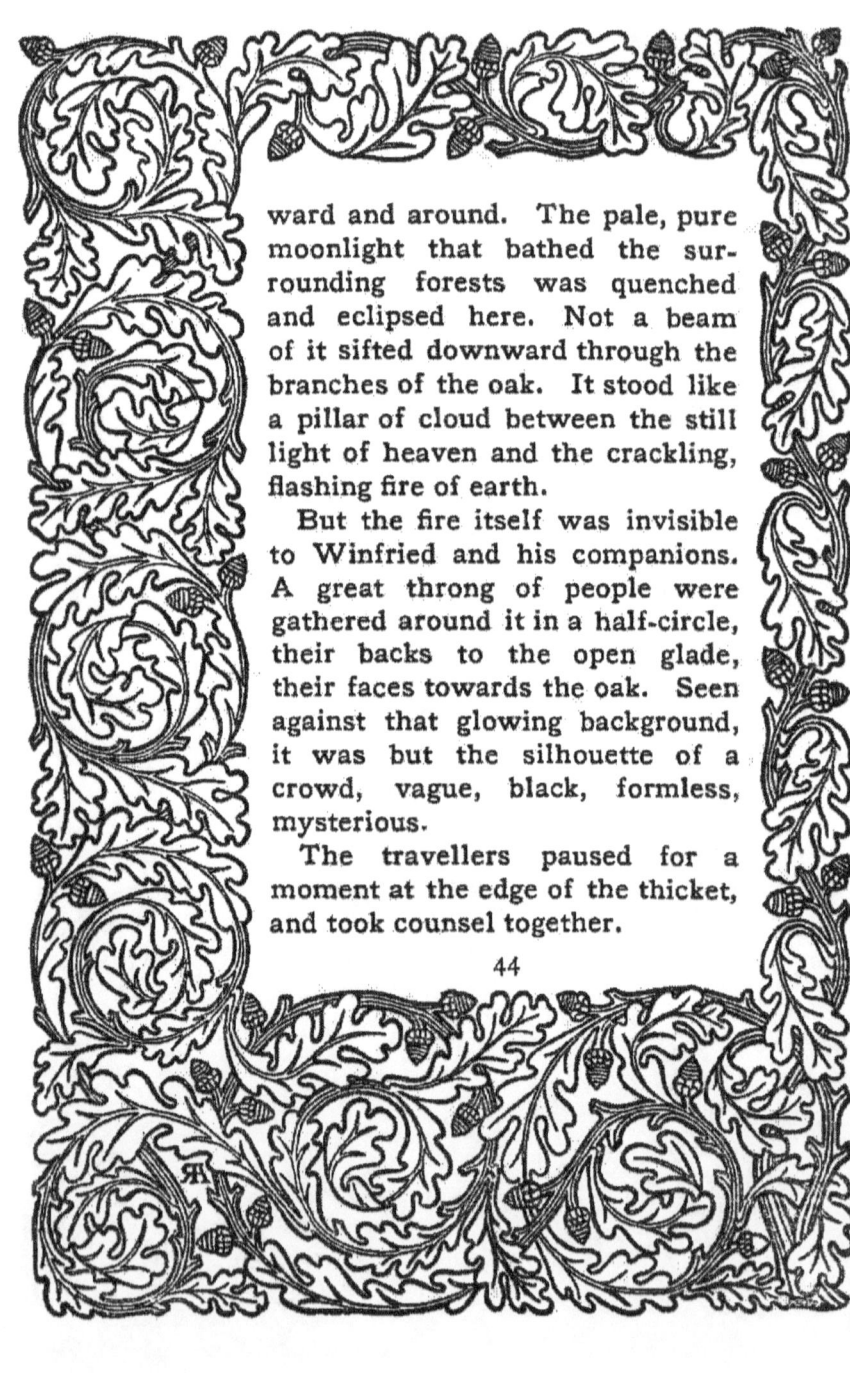

ward and around. The pale, pure
moonlight that bathed the sur-
rounding forests was quenched
and eclipsed here. Not a beam
of it sifted downward through the
branches of the oak. It stood like
a pillar of cloud between the still
light of heaven and the crackling,
flashing fire of earth.

But the fire itself was invisible
to Winfried and his companions.
A great throng of people were
gathered around it in a half-circle,
their backs to the open glade,
their faces towards the oak. Seen
against that glowing background,
it was but the silhouette of a
crowd, vague, black, formless,
mysterious.

The travellers paused for a
moment at the edge of the thicket,
and took counsel together.

44

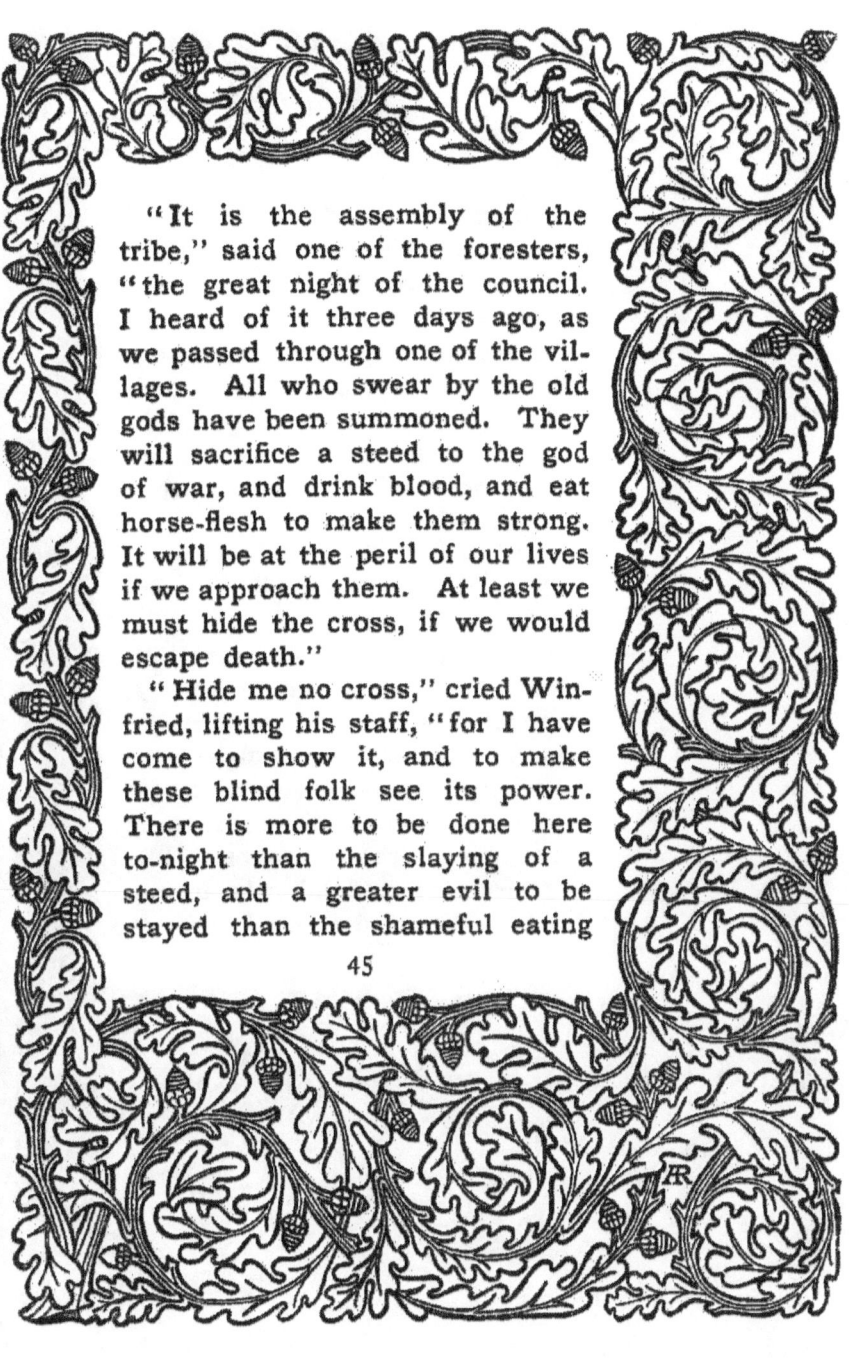

"It is the assembly of the tribe," said one of the foresters, "the great night of the council. I heard of it three days ago, as we passed through one of the villages. All who swear by the old gods have been summoned. They will sacrifice a steed to the god of war, and drink blood, and eat horse-flesh to make them strong. It will be at the peril of our lives if we approach them. At least we must hide the cross, if we would escape death."

"Hide me no cross," cried Winfried, lifting his staff, "for I have come to show it, and to make these blind folk see its power. There is more to be done here to-night than the slaying of a steed, and a greater evil to be stayed than the shameful eating

45

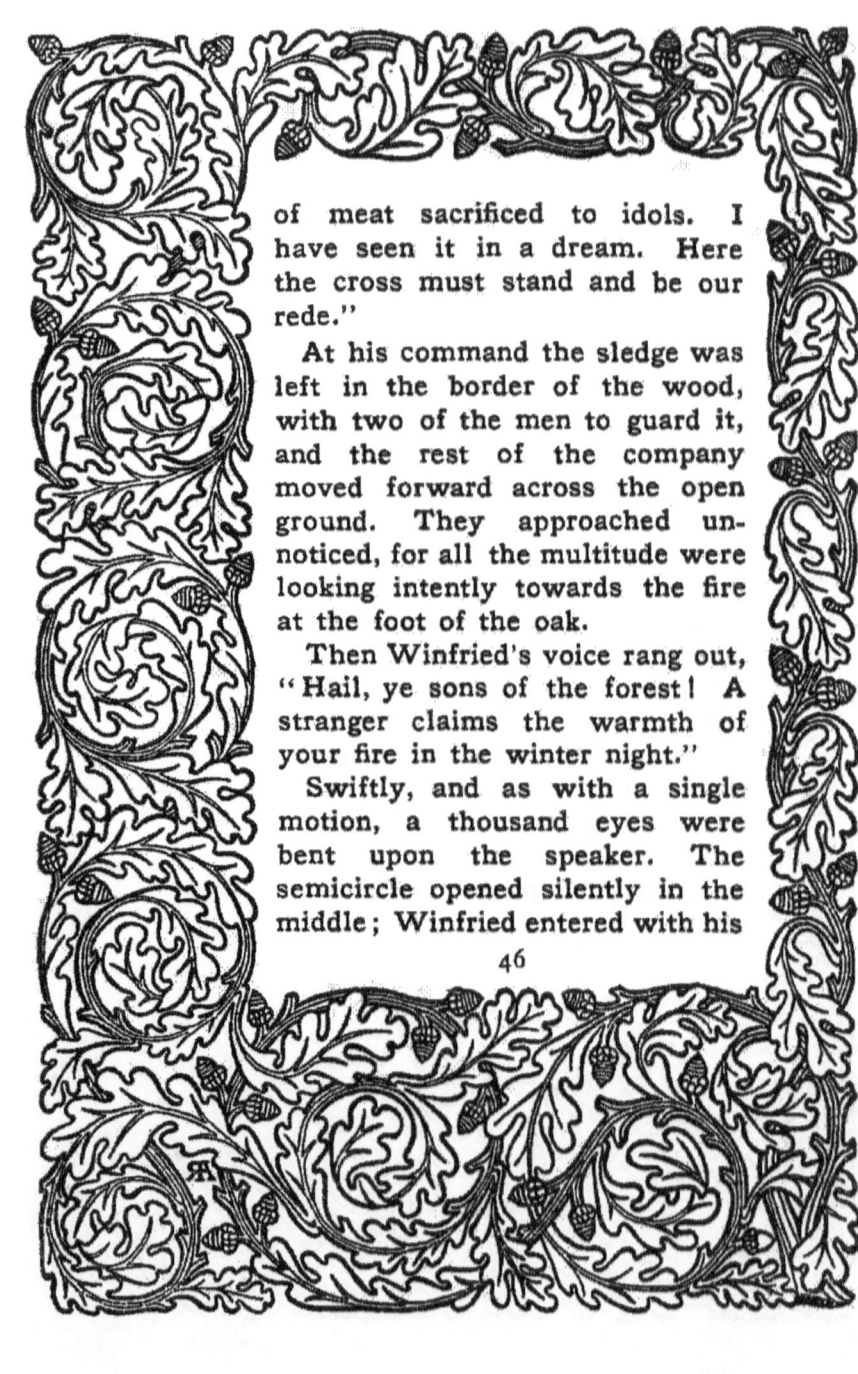

of meat sacrificed to idols. I
have seen it in a dream. Here
the cross must stand and be our
rede.''

At his command the sledge was
left in the border of the wood,
with two of the men to guard it,
and the rest of the company
moved forward across the open
ground. They approached un-
noticed, for all the multitude were
looking intently towards the fire
at the foot of the oak.

Then Winfried's voice rang out,
"Hail, ye sons of the forest! A
stranger claims the warmth of
your fire in the winter night.''

Swiftly, and as with a single
motion, a thousand eyes were
bent upon the speaker. The
semicircle opened silently in the
middle; Winfried entered with his

46

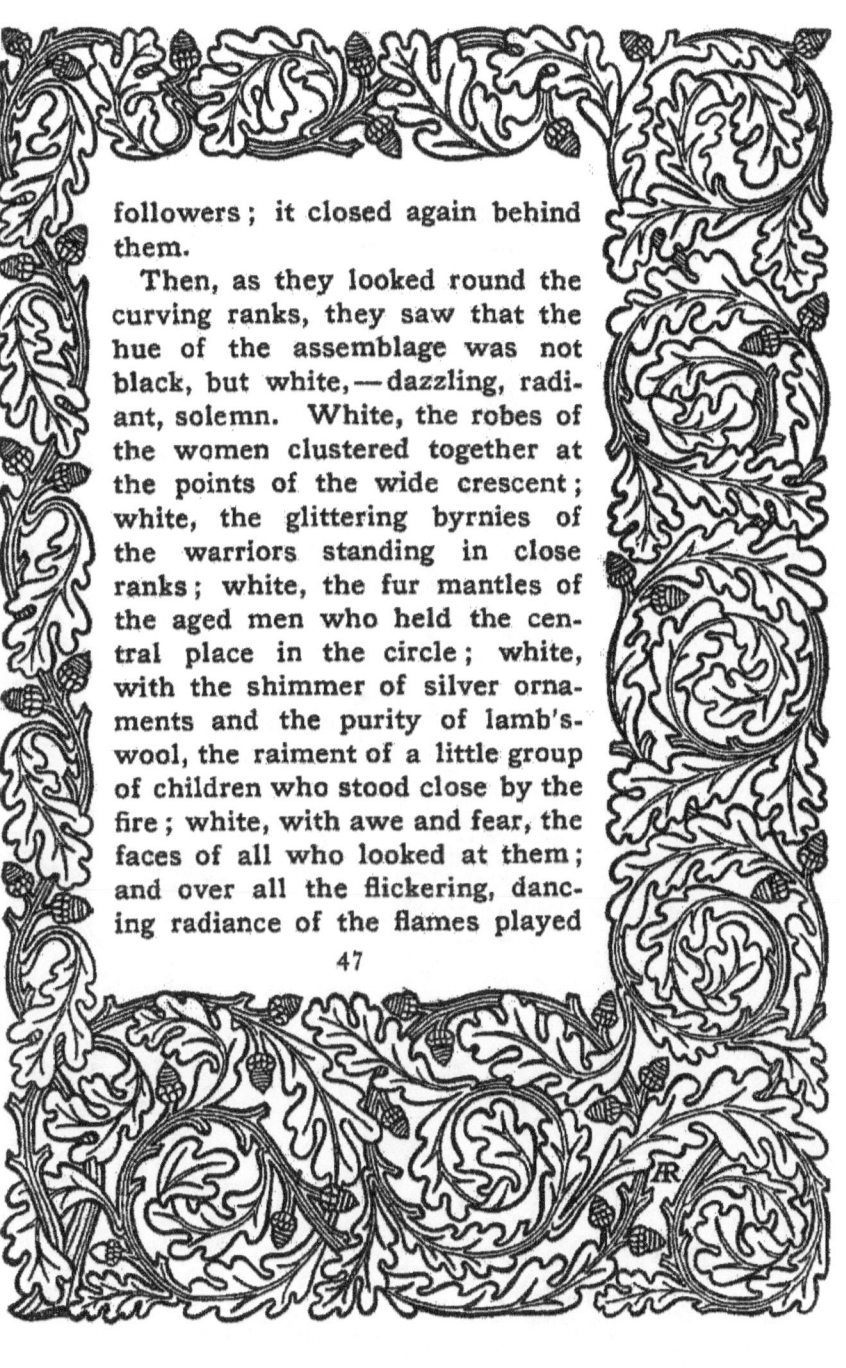

followers; it closed again behind them.

Then, as they looked round the curving ranks, they saw that the hue of the assemblage was not black, but white, — dazzling, radiant, solemn. White, the robes of the women clustered together at the points of the wide crescent; white, the glittering byrnies of the warriors standing in close ranks; white, the fur mantles of the aged men who held the central place in the circle; white, with the shimmer of silver ornaments and the purity of lamb's-wool, the raiment of a little group of children who stood close by the fire; white, with awe and fear, the faces of all who looked at them; and over all the flickering, dancing radiance of the flames played

47

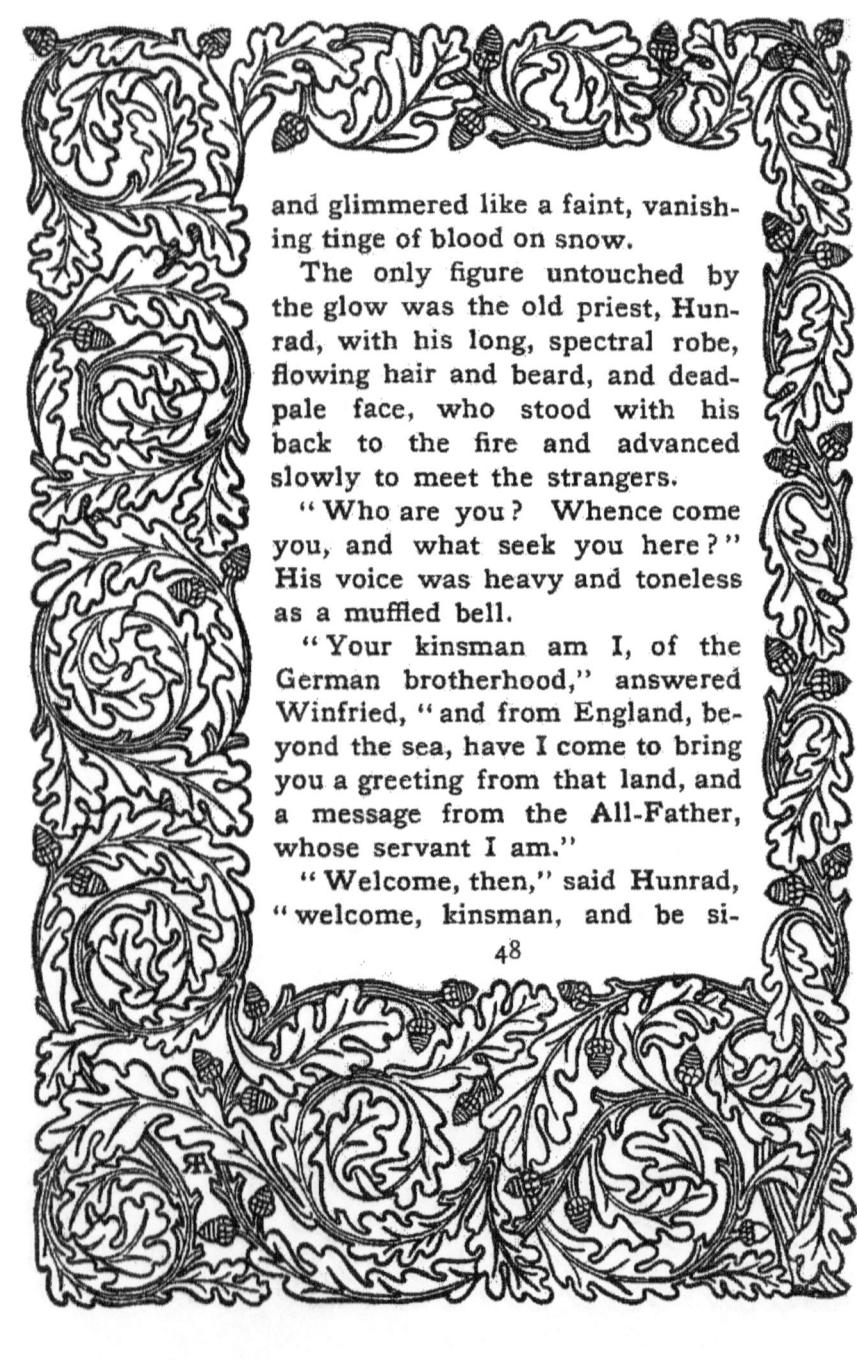

and glimmered like a faint, vanishing tinge of blood on snow.

The only figure untouched by the glow was the old priest, Hunrad, with his long, spectral robe, flowing hair and beard, and deadpale face, who stood with his back to the fire and advanced slowly to meet the strangers.

"Who are you? Whence come you, and what seek you here?" His voice was heavy and toneless as a muffled bell.

"Your kinsman am I, of the German brotherhood," answered Winfried, "and from England, beyond the sea, have I come to bring you a greeting from that land, and a message from the All-Father, whose servant I am."

"Welcome, then," said Hunrad, "welcome, kinsman, and be si-

48

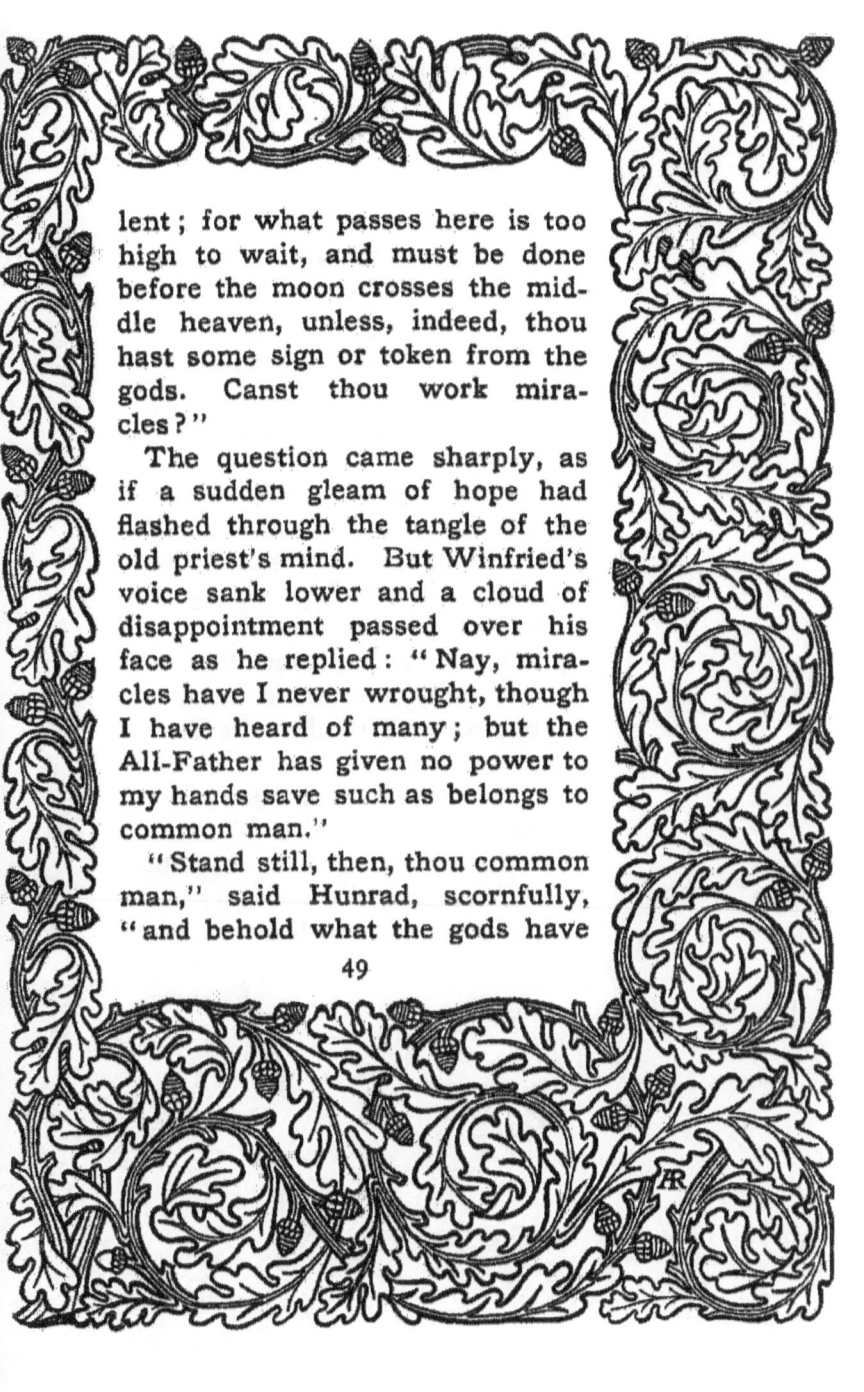

lent; for what passes here is too high to wait, and must be done before the moon crosses the middle heaven, unless, indeed, thou hast some sign or token from the gods. Canst thou work miracles?"

The question came sharply, as if a sudden gleam of hope had flashed through the tangle of the old priest's mind. But Winfried's voice sank lower and a cloud of disappointment passed over his face as he replied: "Nay, miracles have I never wrought, though I have heard of many; but the All-Father has given no power to my hands save such as belongs to common man."

"Stand still, then, thou common man," said Hunrad, scornfully, "and behold what the gods have

49

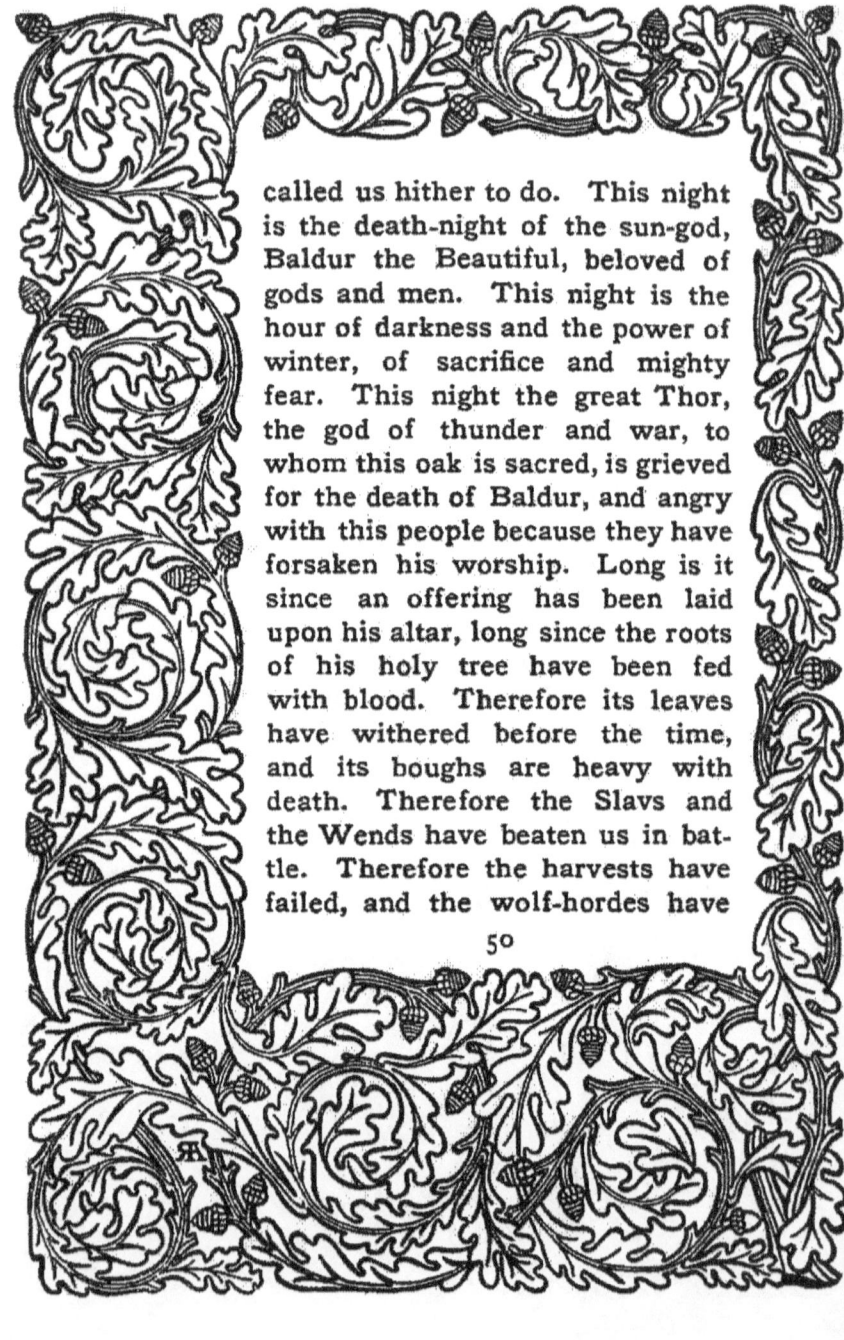

called us hither to do. This night
is the death-night of the sun-god,
Baldur the Beautiful, beloved of
gods and men. This night is the
hour of darkness and the power of
winter, of sacrifice and mighty
fear. This night the great Thor,
the god of thunder and war, to
whom this oak is sacred, is grieved
for the death of Baldur, and angry
with this people because they have
forsaken his worship. Long is it
since an offering has been laid
upon his altar, long since the roots
of his holy tree have been fed
with blood. Therefore its leaves
have withered before the time,
and its boughs are heavy with
death. Therefore the Slavs and
the Wends have beaten us in battle. Therefore the harvests have
failed, and the wolf-hordes have

50

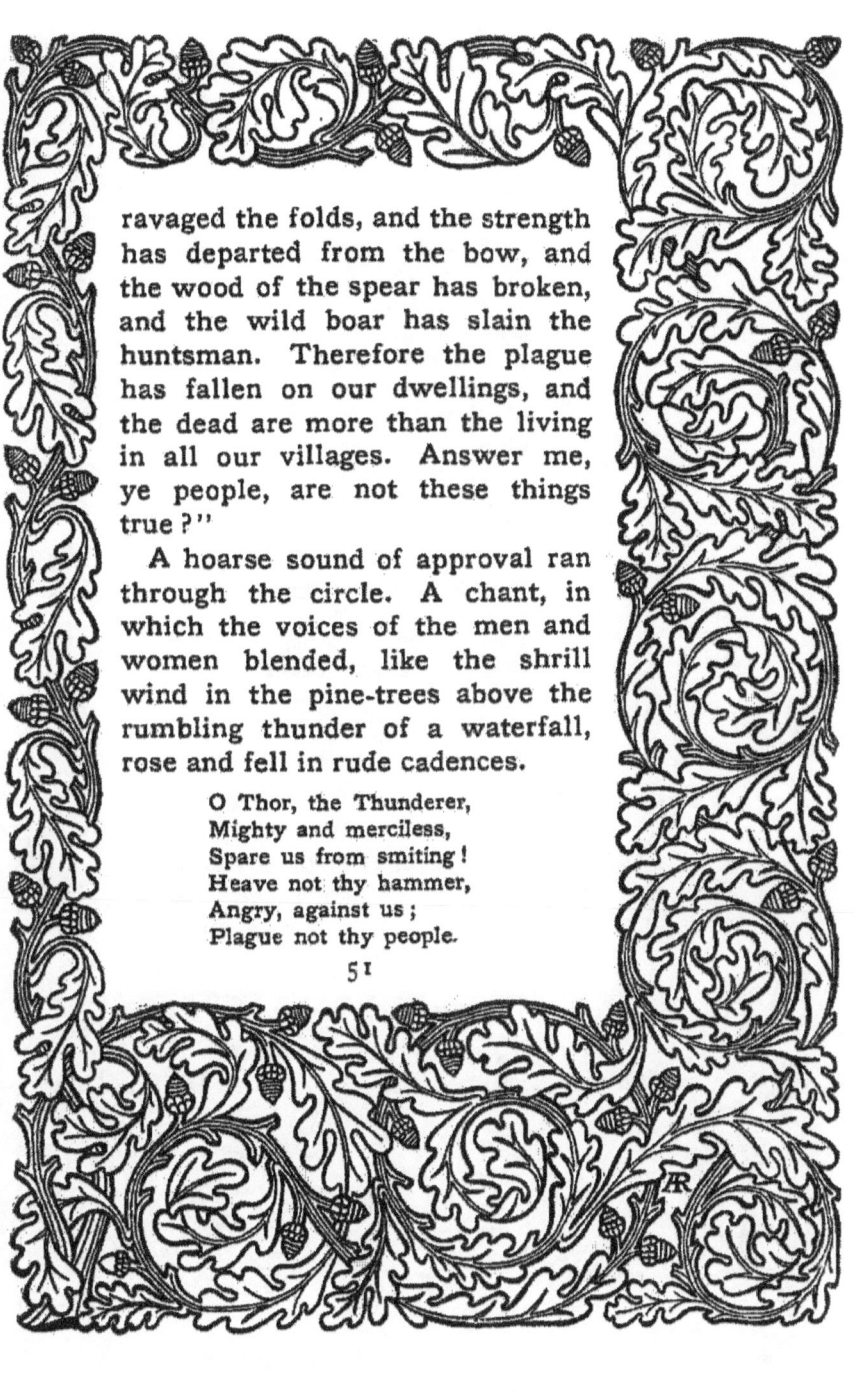

ravaged the folds, and the strength
has departed from the bow, and
the wood of the spear has broken,
and the wild boar has slain the
huntsman. Therefore the plague
has fallen on our dwellings, and
the dead are more than the living
in all our villages. Answer me,
ye people, are not these things
true ?''

A hoarse sound of approval ran
through the circle. A chant, in
which the voices of the men and
women blended, like the shrill
wind in the pine-trees above the
rumbling thunder of a waterfall,
rose and fell in rude cadences.

O Thor, the Thunderer,
Mighty and merciless,
Spare us from smiting!
Heave not thy hammer,
Angry, against us;
Plague not thy people.

51

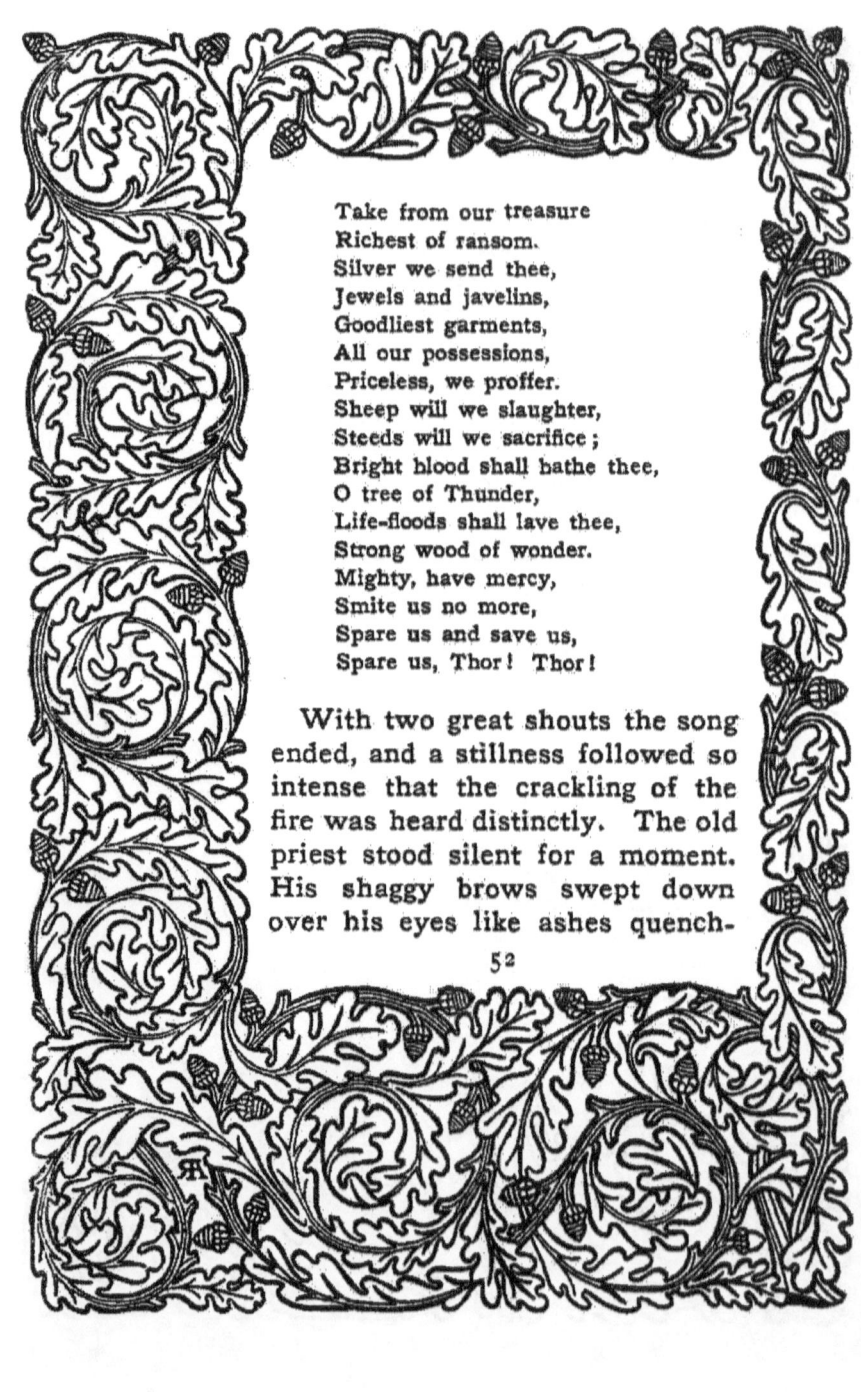

Take from our treasure
Richest of ransom.
Silver we send thee,
Jewels and javelins,
Goodliest garments,
All our possessions,
Priceless, we proffer.
Sheep will we slaughter,
Steeds will we sacrifice;
Bright blood shall bathe thee,
O tree of Thunder,
Life-floods shall lave thee,
Strong wood of wonder.
Mighty, have mercy,
Smite us no more,
Spare us and save us,
Spare us, Thor! Thor!

With two great shouts the song
ended, and a stillness followed so
intense that the crackling of the
fire was heard distinctly. The old
priest stood silent for a moment.
His shaggy brows swept down
over his eyes like ashes quench-

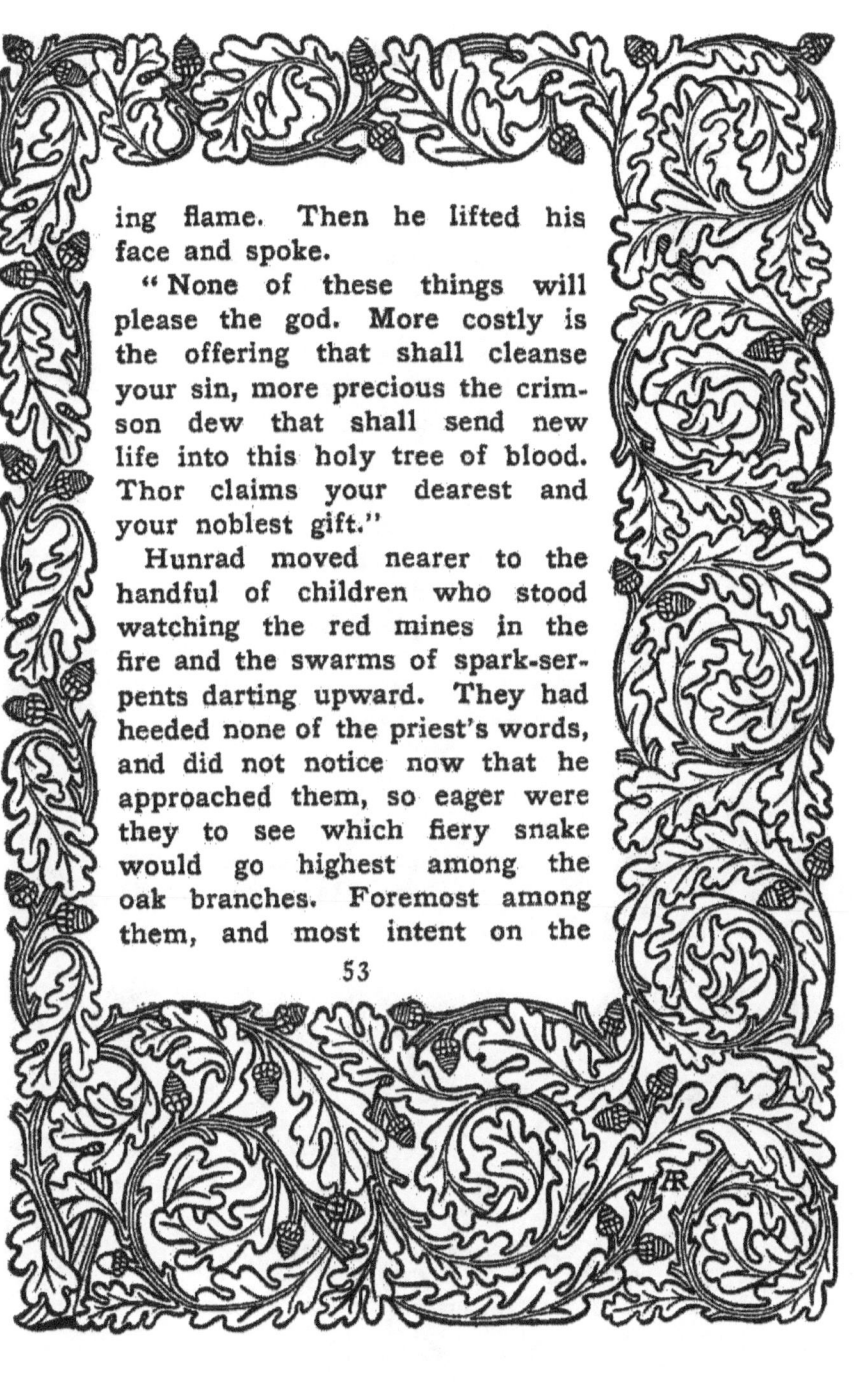

ing flame. Then he lifted his
face and spoke.

"None of these things will
please the god. More costly is
the offering that shall cleanse
your sin, more precious the crimson dew that shall send new
life into this holy tree of blood.
Thor claims your dearest and
your noblest gift."

Hunrad moved nearer to the
handful of children who stood
watching the red mines in the
fire and the swarms of spark-ser-
pents darting upward. They had
heeded none of the priest's words,
and did not notice now that he
approached them, so eager were
they to see which fiery snake
would go highest among the
oak branches. Foremost among
them, and most intent on the

53

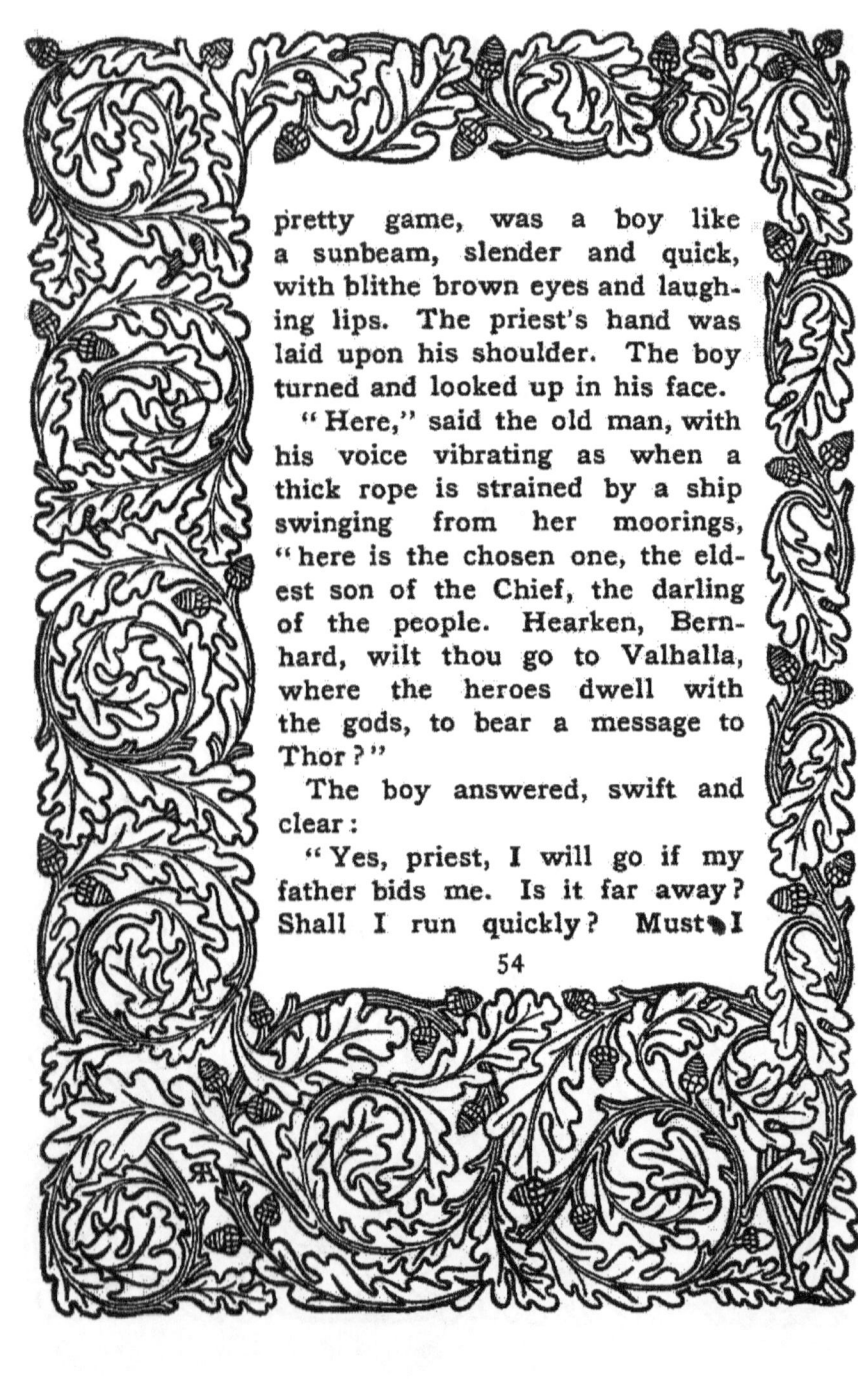

pretty game, was a boy like
a sunbeam, slender and quick,
with blithe brown eyes and laugh-
ing lips. The priest's hand was
laid upon his shoulder. The boy
turned and looked up in his face.

"Here," said the old man, with
his voice vibrating as when a
thick rope is strained by a ship
swinging from her moorings,
"here is the chosen one, the eld-
est son of the Chief, the darling
of the people. Hearken, Bernhard, wilt thou go to Valhalla,
where the heroes dwell with
the gods, to bear a message to
Thor?"

The boy answered, swift and
clear:

"Yes, priest, I will go if my
father bids me. Is it far away?
Shall I run quickly? Must I

54

take my bow and arrows for the
wolves?"

The boy's father, the Chieftain Gundhar, standing among his
bearded warriors, drew his breath
deep, and leaned so heavily on
the handle of his spear that the
wood cracked. And his wife,
Irma, bending forward from the
ranks of women, pushed the golden
hair from her forehead with one
hand. The other dragged at the
silver chain about her neck until
the rough links pierced her flesh,
and the red drops fell unheeded
on the snow of her breast.

A sigh passed through the
crowd, like the murmur of the
forest before the storm breaks.
Yet no one spoke save Hunrad:

"Yes, my Prince, both bow and
spear shalt thou have, for the

55

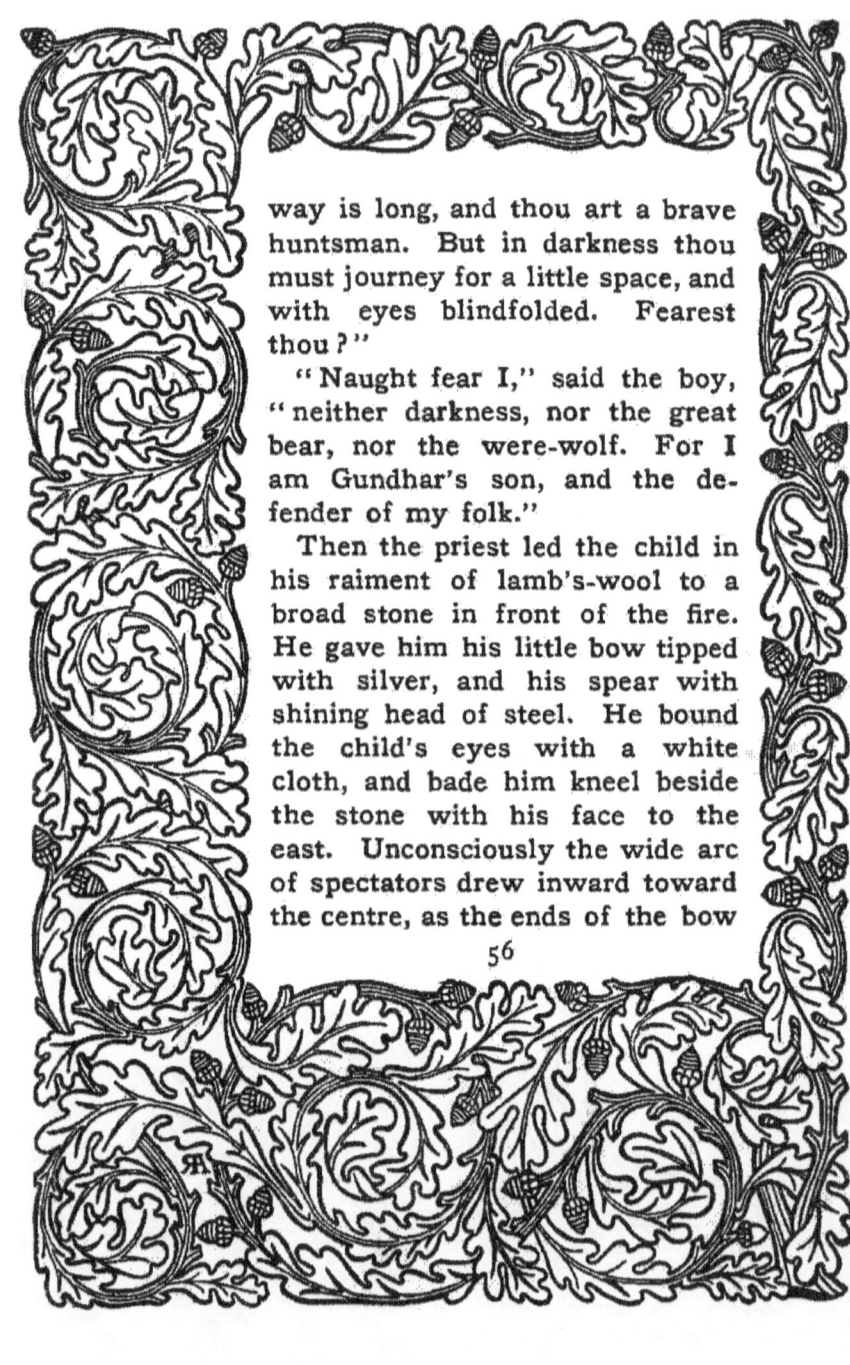

way is long, and thou art a brave huntsman. But in darkness thou must journey for a little space, and with eyes blindfolded. Fearest thou?"

"Naught fear I," said the boy, "neither darkness, nor the great bear, nor the were-wolf. For I am Gundhar's son, and the defender of my folk."

Then the priest led the child in his raiment of lamb's-wool to a broad stone in front of the fire. He gave him his little bow tipped with silver, and his spear with shining head of steel. He bound the child's eyes with a white cloth, and bade him kneel beside the stone with his face to the east. Unconsciously the wide arc of spectators drew inward toward the centre, as the ends of the bow

56

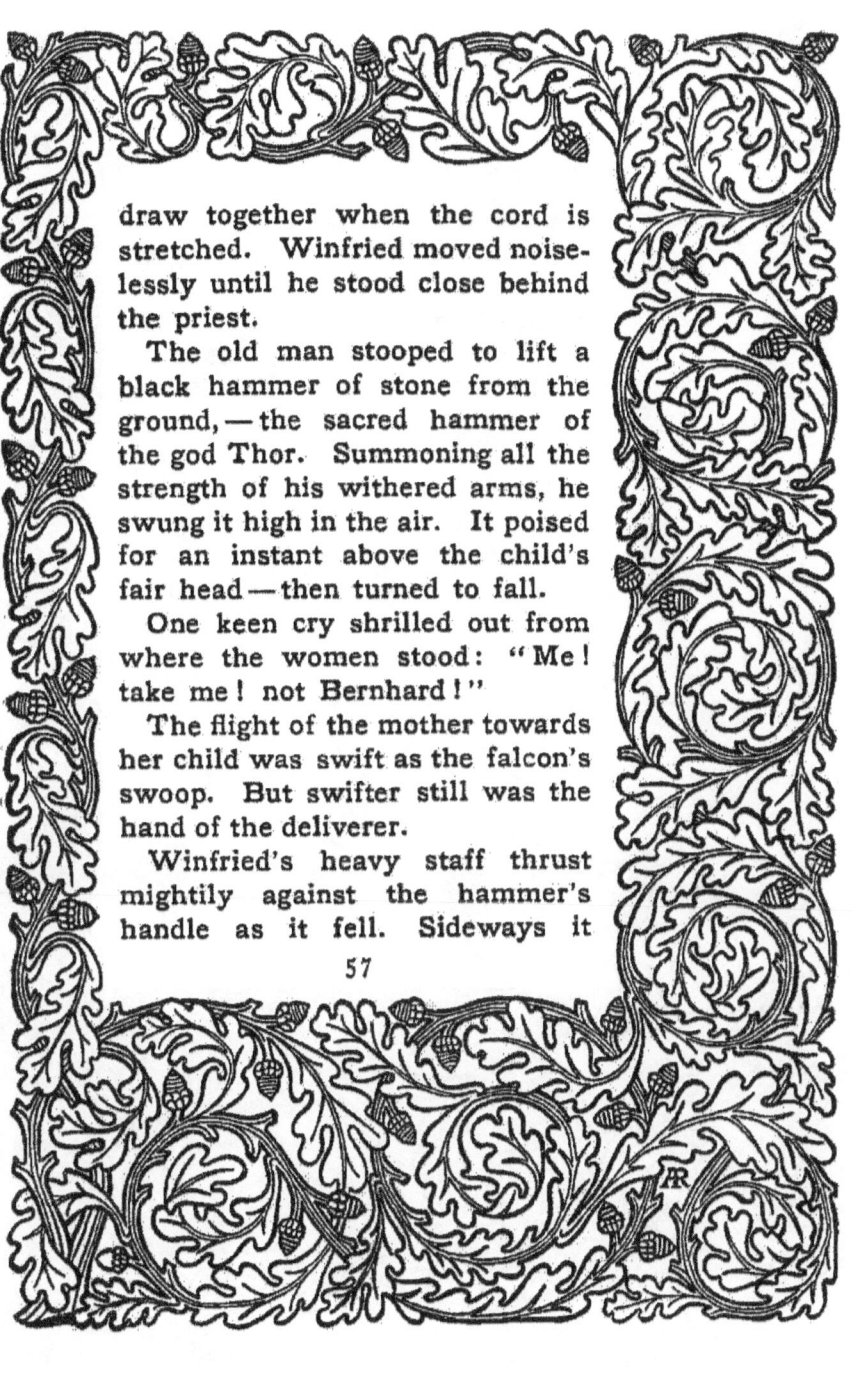

draw together when the cord is
stretched. Winfried moved noise-
lessly until he stood close behind
the priest.

The old man stooped to lift a
black hammer of stone from the
ground, — the sacred hammer of
the god Thor. Summoning all the
strength of his withered arms, he
swung it high in the air. It poised
for an instant above the child's
fair head — then turned to fall.

One keen cry shrilled out from
where the women stood: "Me!
take me! not Bernhard!"

The flight of the mother towards
her child was swift as the falcon's
swoop. But swifter still was the
hand of the deliverer.

Winfried's heavy staff thrust
mightily against the hammer's
handle as it fell. Sideways it

57

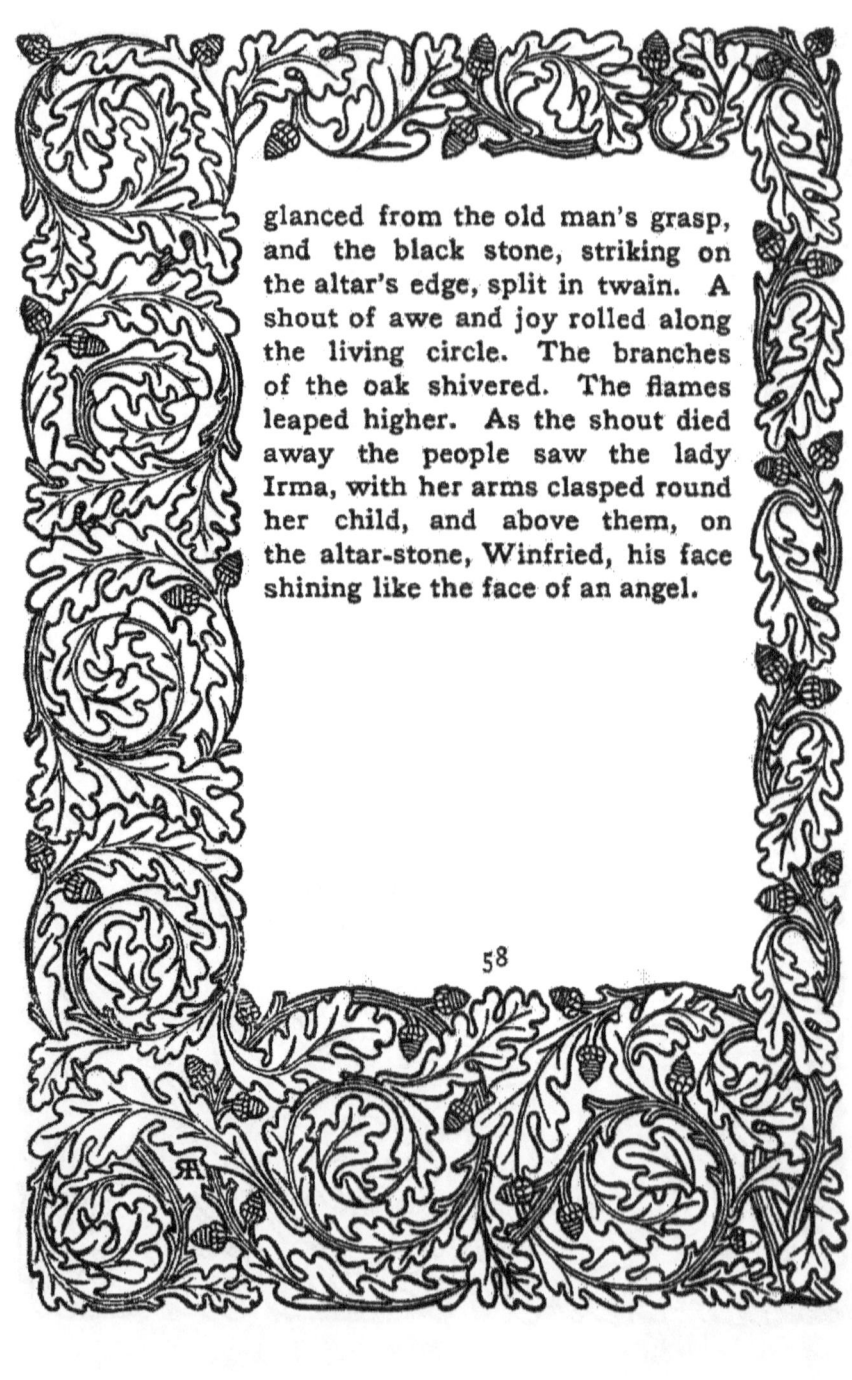

glanced from the old man's grasp,
and the black stone, striking on
the altar's edge, split in twain. A
shout of awe and joy rolled along
the living circle. The branches
of the oak shivered. The flames
leaped higher. As the shout died
away the people saw the lady
Irma, with her arms clasped round
her child, and above them, on
the altar-stone, Winfried, his face
shining like the face of an angel.

58

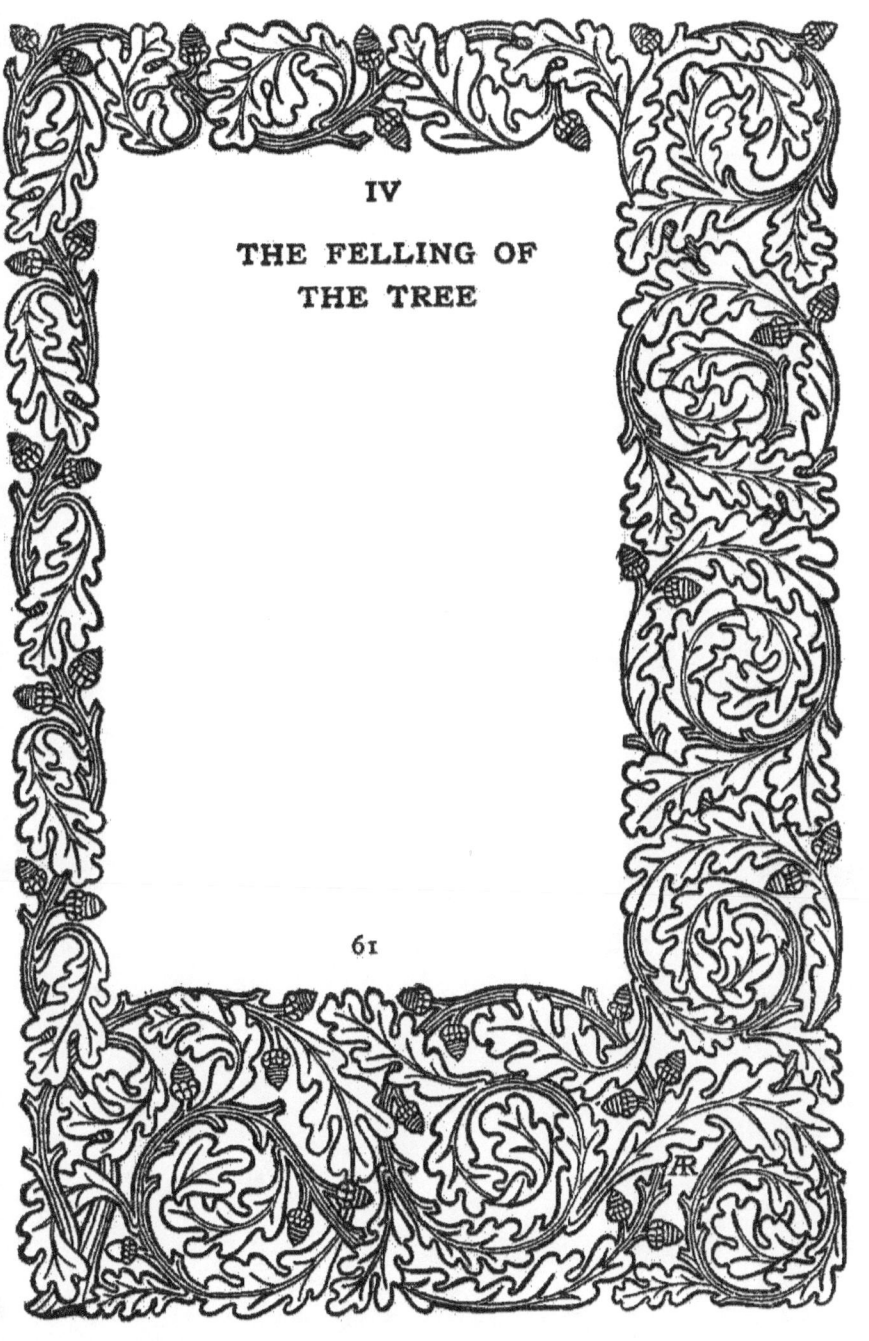

IV

THE FELLING OF
THE TREE

61

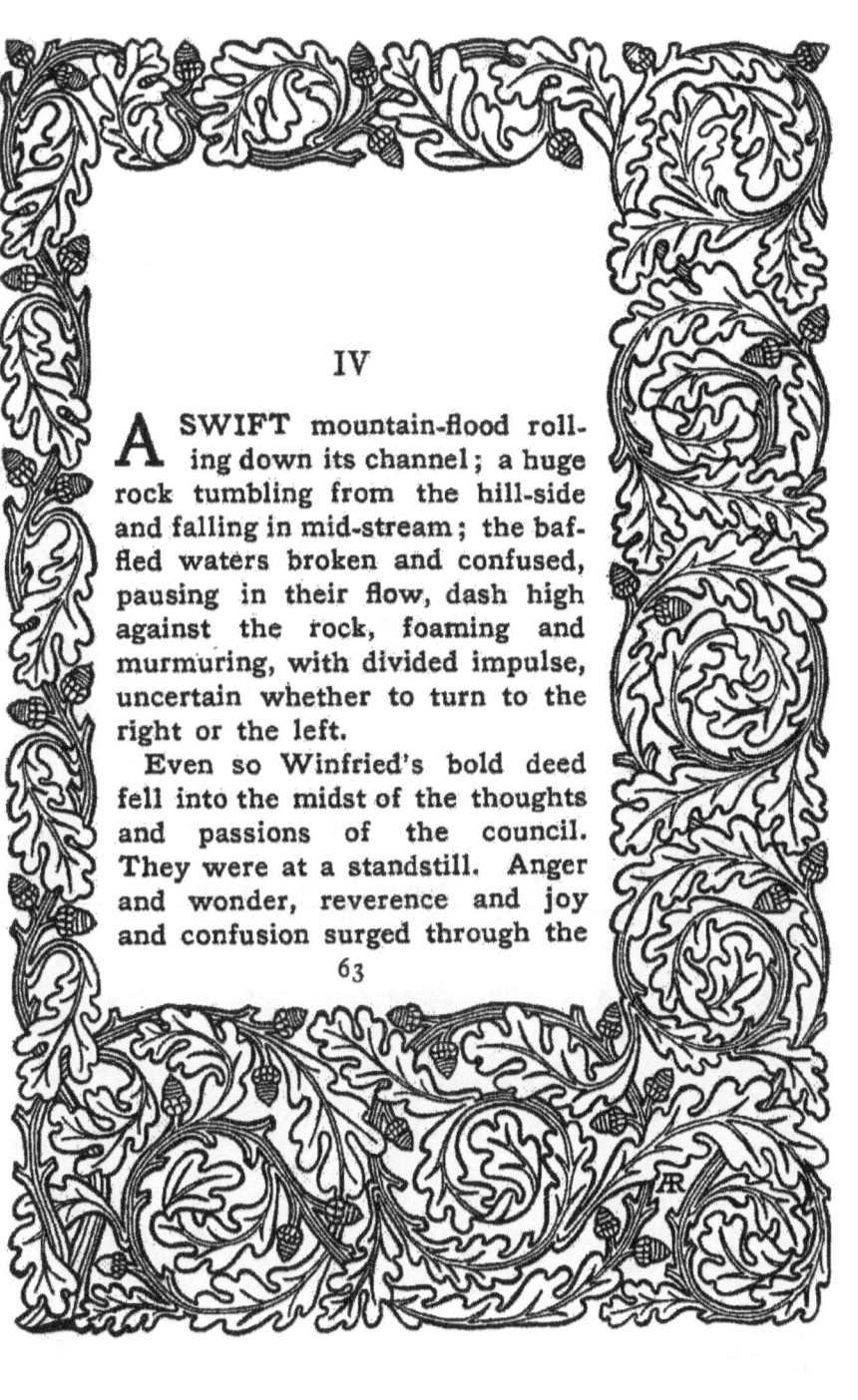

IV

A SWIFT mountain-flood rolling down its channel; a huge
rock tumbling from the hill-side
and falling in mid-stream; the baf-
fled waters broken and confused,
pausing in their flow, dash high
against the rock, foaming and
murmuring, with divided impulse,
uncertain whether to turn to the
right or the left.

Even so Winfried's bold deed
fell into the midst of the thoughts
and passions of the council.
They were at a standstill. Anger
and wonder, reverence and joy
and confusion surged through the

63

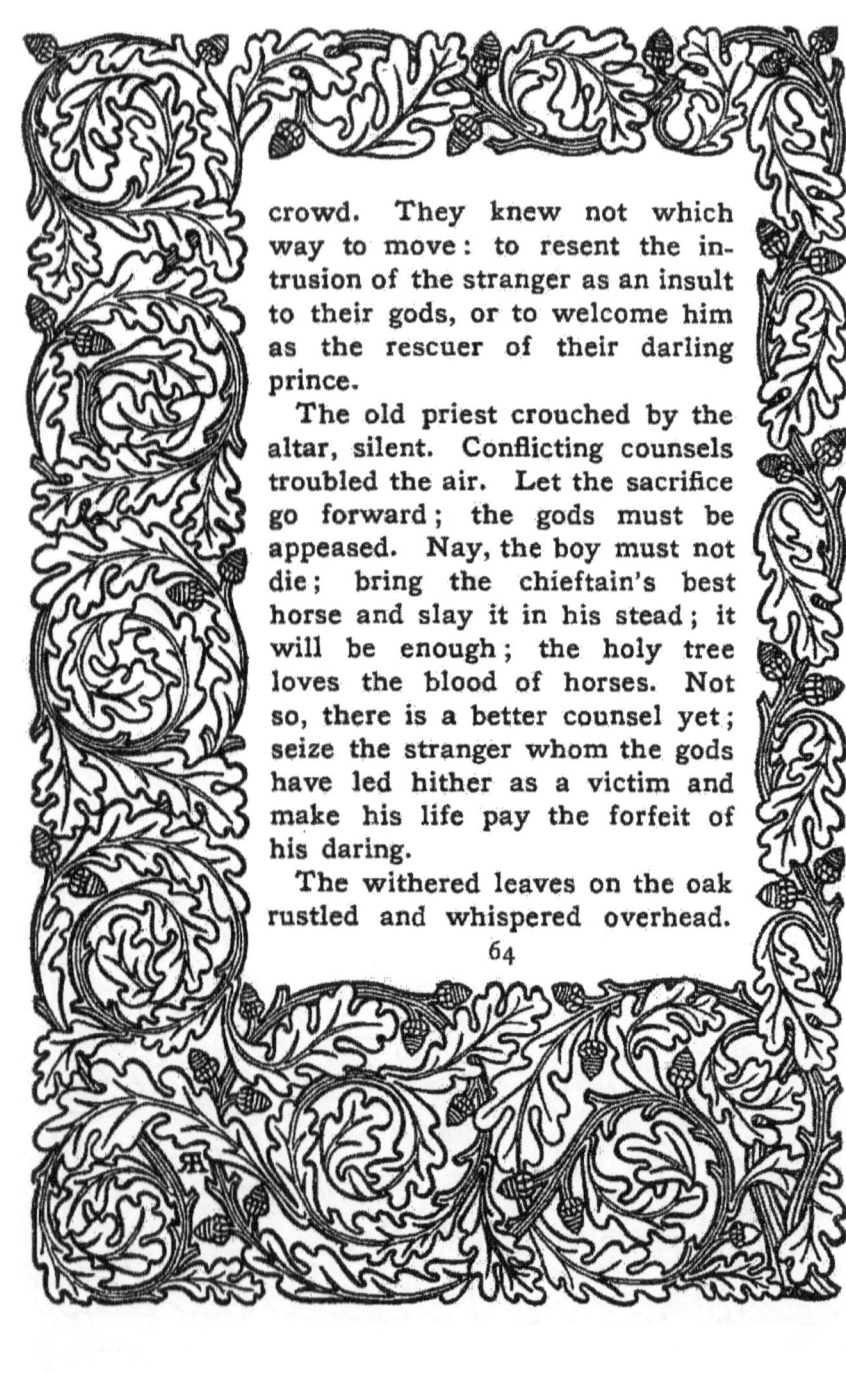

crowd. They knew not which way to move: to resent the intrusion of the stranger as an insult to their gods, or to welcome him as the rescuer of their darling prince.

The old priest crouched by the altar, silent. Conflicting counsels troubled the air. Let the sacrifice go forward; the gods must be appeased. Nay, the boy must not die; bring the chieftain's best horse and slay it in his stead; it will be enough; the holy tree loves the blood of horses. Not so, there is a better counsel yet; seize the stranger whom the gods have led hither as a victim and make his life pay the forfeit of his daring.

The withered leaves on the oak rustled and whispered overhead.

64

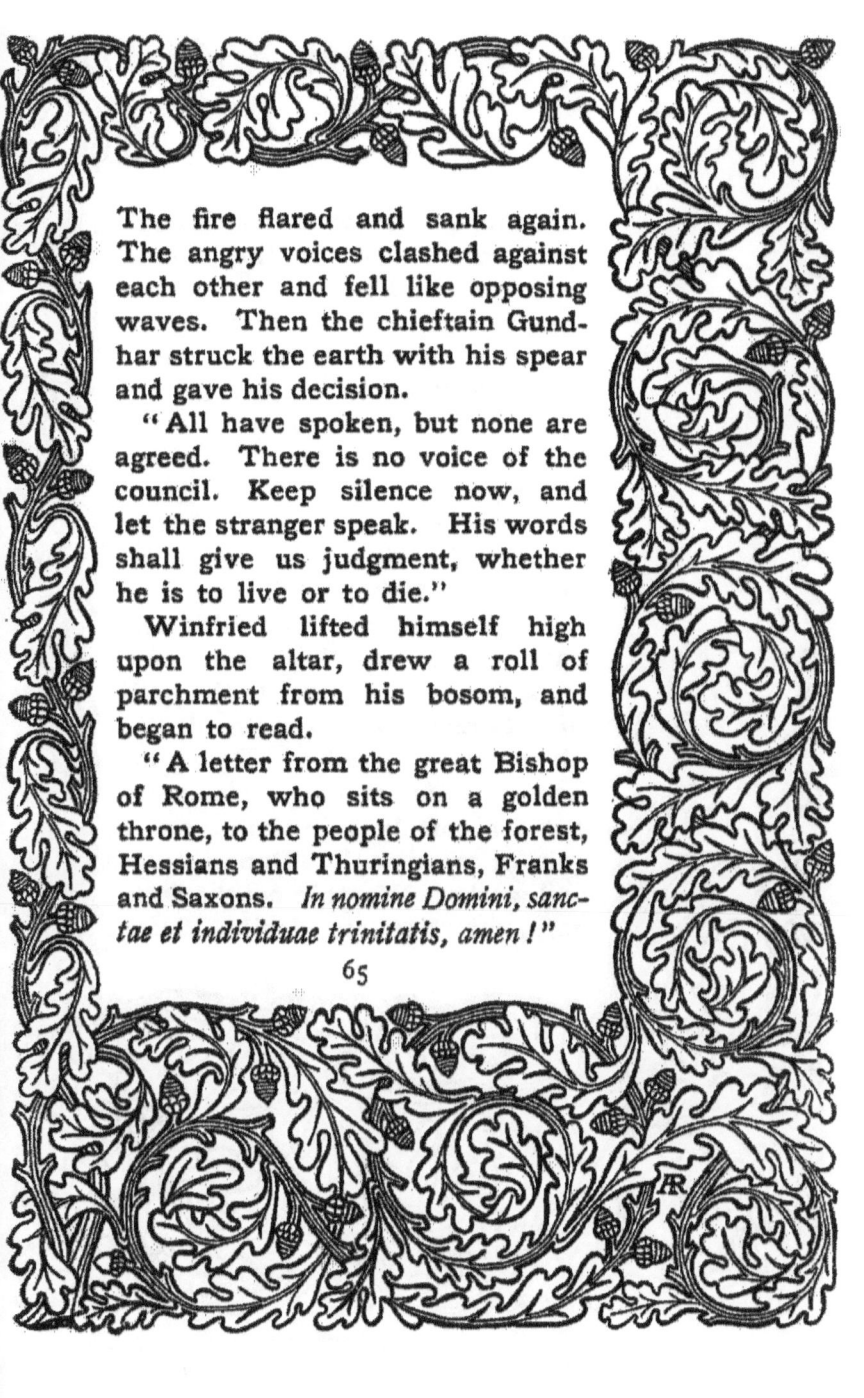

The fire flared and sank again. The angry voices clashed against each other and fell like opposing waves. Then the chieftain Gundhar struck the earth with his spear and gave his decision.

"All have spoken, but none are agreed. There is no voice of the council. Keep silence now, and let the stranger speak. His words shall give us judgment, whether he is to live or to die."

Winfried lifted himself high upon the altar, drew a roll of parchment from his bosom, and began to read.

"A letter from the great Bishop of Rome, who sits on a golden throne, to the people of the forest, Hessians and Thuringians, Franks and Saxons. *In nomine Domini, sanctae et individuae trinitatis, amen!*"

65

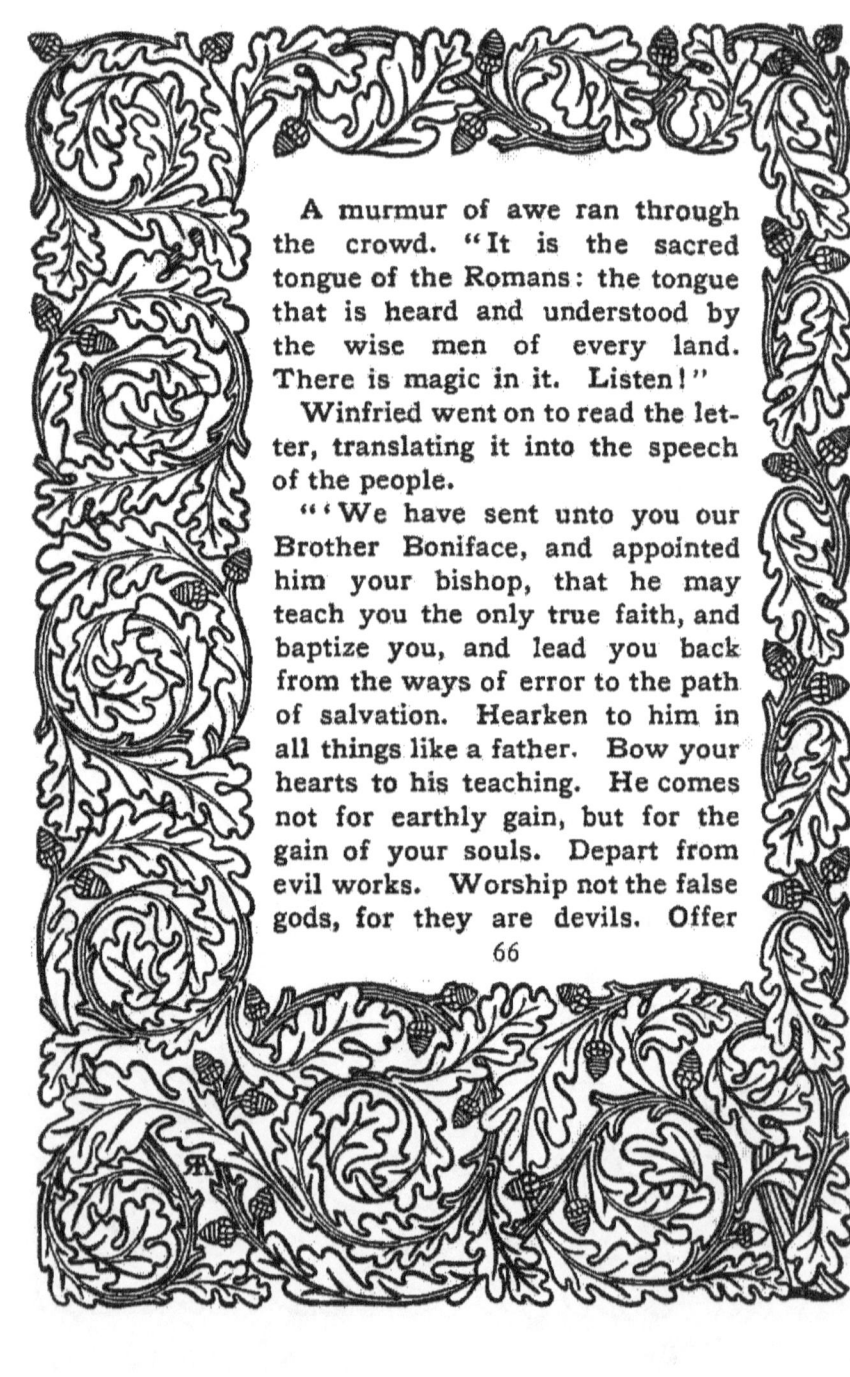

A murmur of awe ran through the crowd. "It is the sacred tongue of the Romans: the tongue that is heard and understood by the wise men of every land. There is magic in it. Listen!"

Winfried went on to read the letter, translating it into the speech of the people.

"'We have sent unto you our Brother Boniface, and appointed him your bishop, that he may teach you the only true faith, and baptize you, and lead you back from the ways of error to the path of salvation. Hearken to him in all things like a father. Bow your hearts to his teaching. He comes not for earthly gain, but for the gain of your souls. Depart from evil works. Worship not the false gods, for they are devils. Offer

66

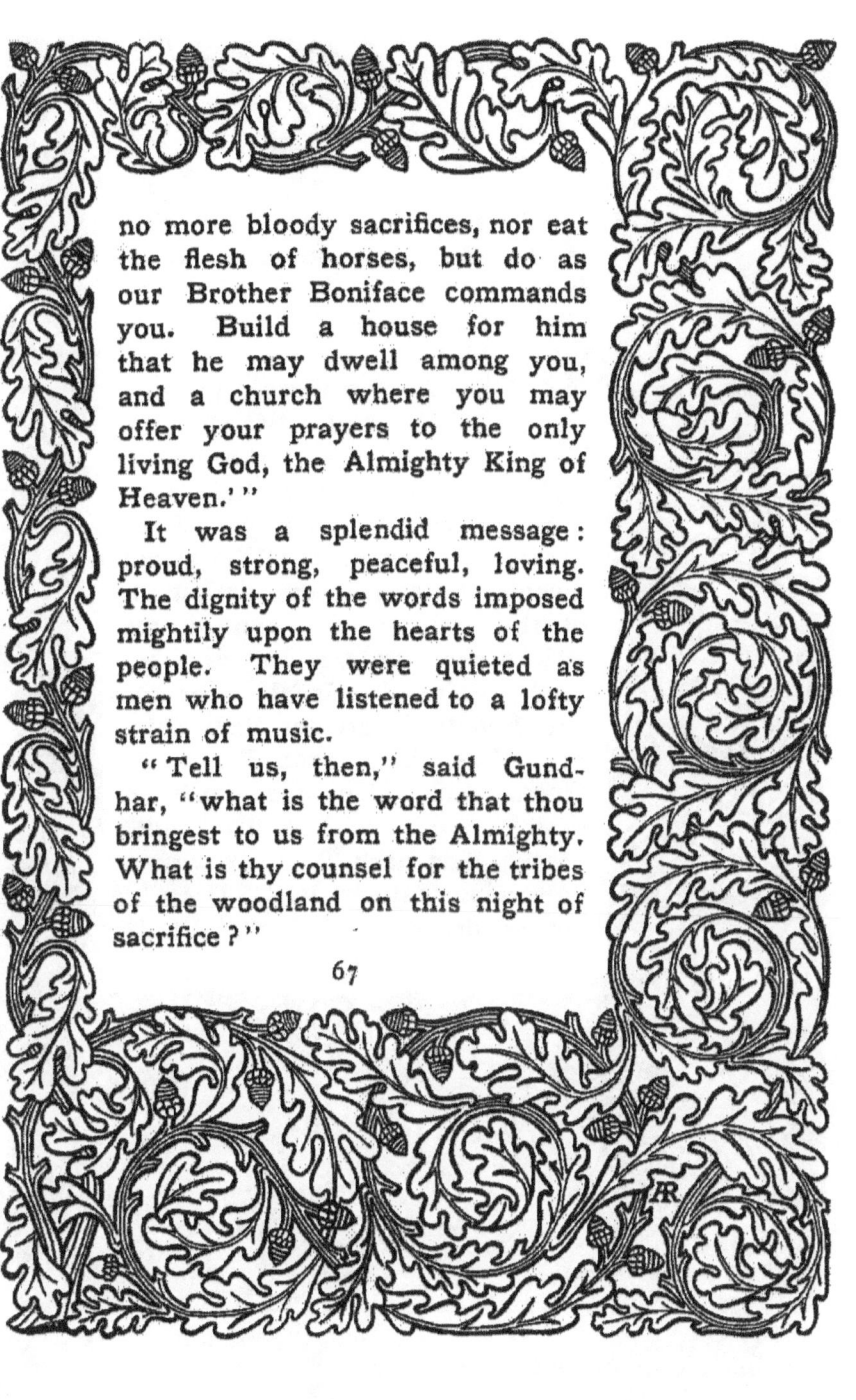

no more bloody sacrifices, nor eat the flesh of horses, but do as our Brother Boniface commands you. Build a house for him that he may dwell among you, and a church where you may offer your prayers to the only living God, the Almighty King of Heaven.'"

It was a splendid message: proud, strong, peaceful, loving. The dignity of the words imposed mightily upon the hearts of the people. They were quieted as men who have listened to a lofty strain of music.

"Tell us, then," said Gundhar, "what is the word that thou bringest to us from the Almighty. What is thy counsel for the tribes of the woodland on this night of sacrifice?"

67

"This is the word, and this is the counsel," answered Winfried. "Not a drop of blood shall fall to-night, save that which pity has drawn from the breast of your princess, in love for her child. Not a life shall be blotted out in the darkness to-night; but the great shadow of the tree which hides you from the light of heaven shall be swept away. For this is the birth-night of the white Christ, son of the All-Father, and Saviour of mankind. Fairer is He than Baldur the Beautiful, greater than Odin the Wise, kinder than Freya the Good. Since He has come to earth the bloody sacrifices must cease. The dark Thor, on whom you vainly call, is dead. Deep in the shades of Niffelheim he is

68

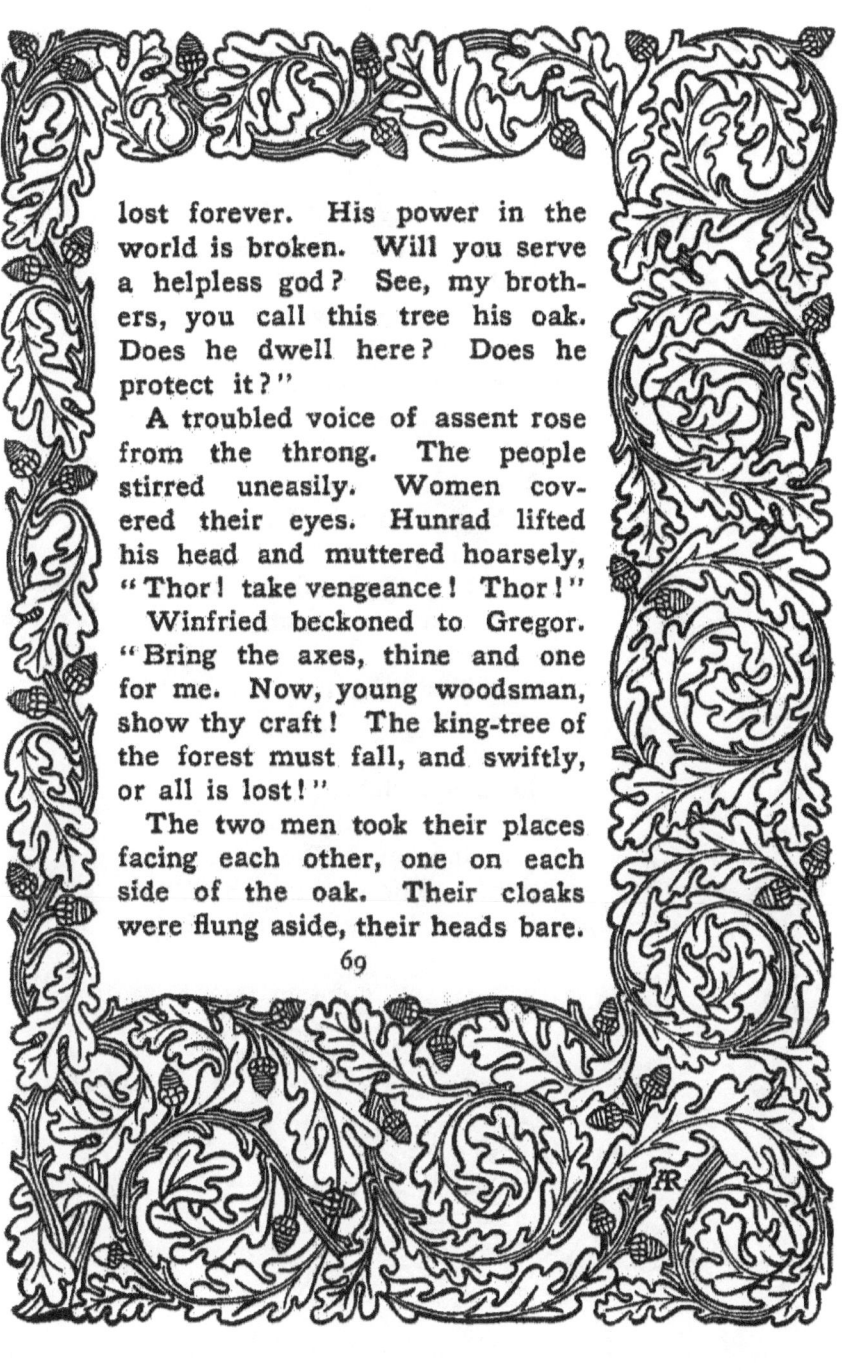

lost forever. His power in the world is broken. Will you serve a helpless god? See, my brothers, you call this tree his oak. Does he dwell here? Does he protect it?"

A troubled voice of assent rose from the throng. The people stirred uneasily. Women covered their eyes. Hunrad lifted his head and muttered hoarsely, "Thor! take vengeance! Thor!"

Winfried beckoned to Gregor. "Bring the axes, thine and one for me. Now, young woodsman, show thy craft! The king-tree of the forest must fall, and swiftly, or all is lost!"

The two men took their places facing each other, one on each side of the oak. Their cloaks were flung aside, their heads bare.

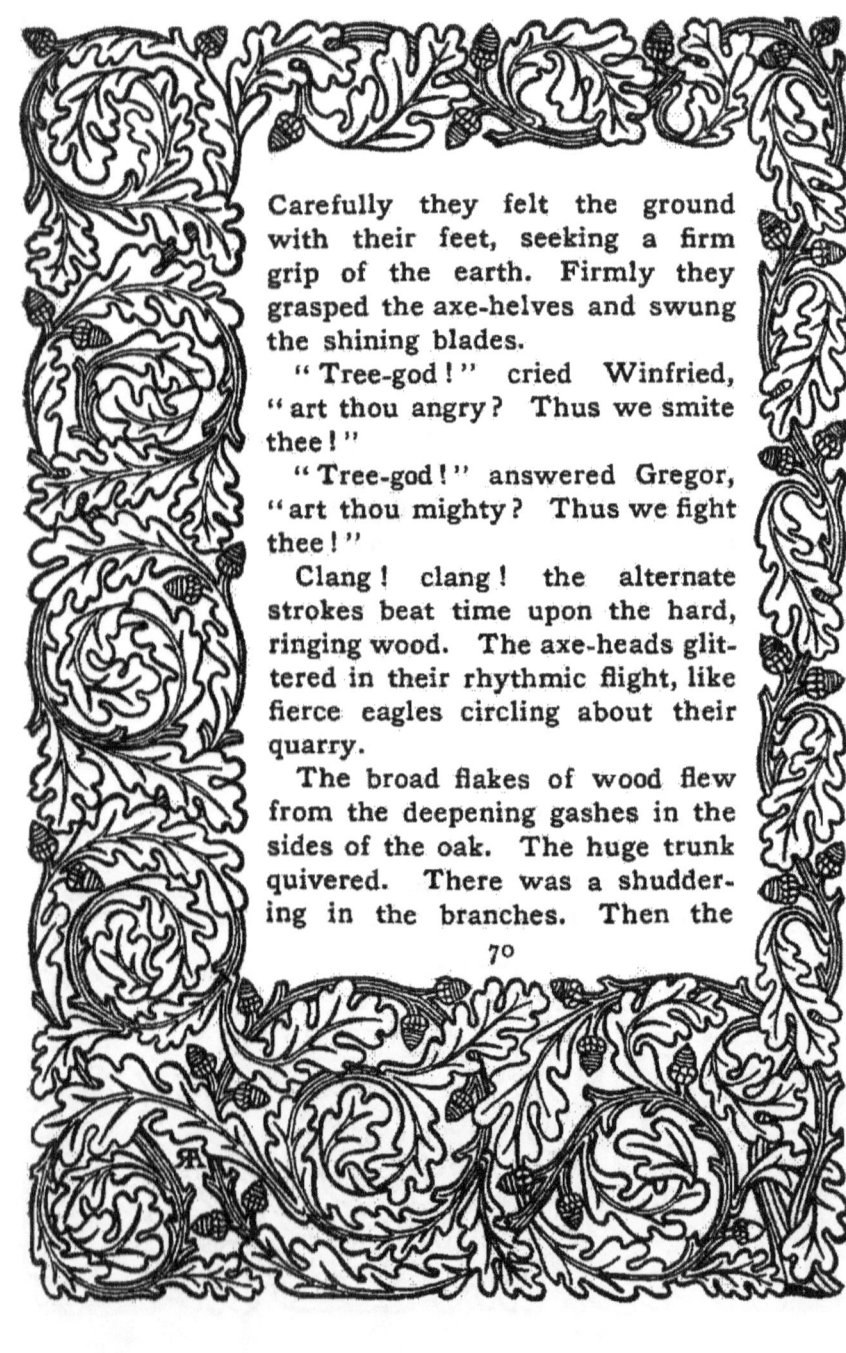

Carefully they felt the ground
with their feet, seeking a firm
grip of the earth. Firmly they
grasped the axe-helves and swung
the shining blades.

"Tree-god!" cried Winfried,
"art thou angry? Thus we smite
thee!"

"Tree-god!" answered Gregor,
"art thou mighty? Thus we fight
thee!"

Clang! clang! the alternate
strokes beat time upon the hard,
ringing wood. The axe-heads glit-
tered in their rhythmic flight, like
fierce eagles circling about their
quarry.

The broad flakes of wood flew
from the deepening gashes in the
sides of the oak. The huge trunk
quivered. There was a shudder-
ing in the branches. Then the

70

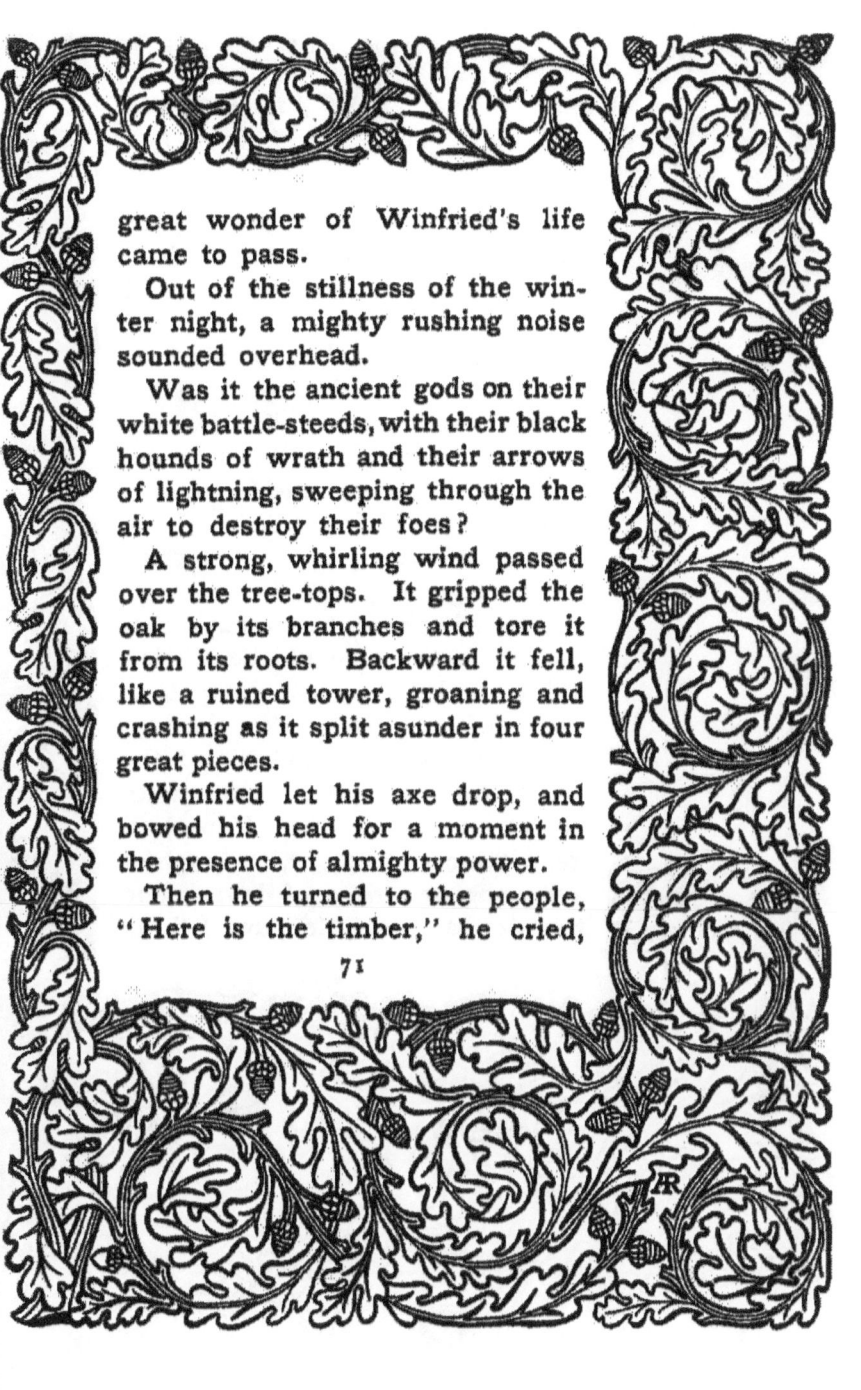

great wonder of Winfried's life came to pass.

Out of the stillness of the winter night, a mighty rushing noise sounded overhead.

Was it the ancient gods on their white battle-steeds, with their black hounds of wrath and their arrows of lightning, sweeping through the air to destroy their foes?

A strong, whirling wind passed over the tree-tops. It gripped the oak by its branches and tore it from its roots. Backward it fell, like a ruined tower, groaning and crashing as it split asunder in four great pieces.

Winfried let his axe drop, and bowed his head for a moment in the presence of almighty power.

Then he turned to the people, "Here is the timber," he cried,

71

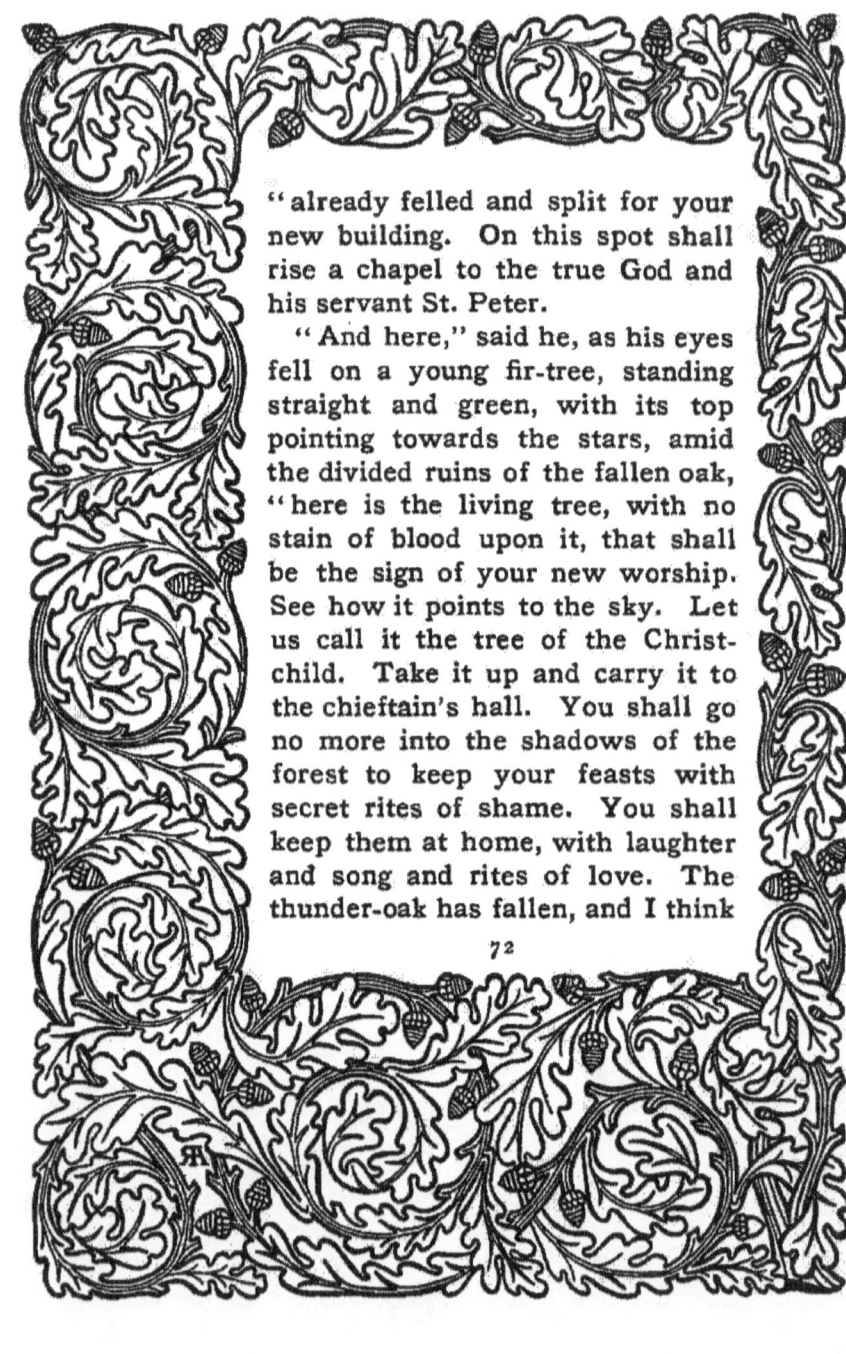

"already felled and split for your new building. On this spot shall rise a chapel to the true God and his servant St. Peter.

"And here," said he, as his eyes fell on a young fir-tree, standing straight and green, with its top pointing towards the stars, amid the divided ruins of the fallen oak, "here is the living tree, with no stain of blood upon it, that shall be the sign of your new worship. See how it points to the sky. Let us call it the tree of the Christ-child. Take it up and carry it to the chieftain's hall. You shall go no more into the shadows of the forest to keep your feasts with secret rites of shame. You shall keep them at home, with laughter and song and rites of love. The thunder-oak has fallen, and I think

72

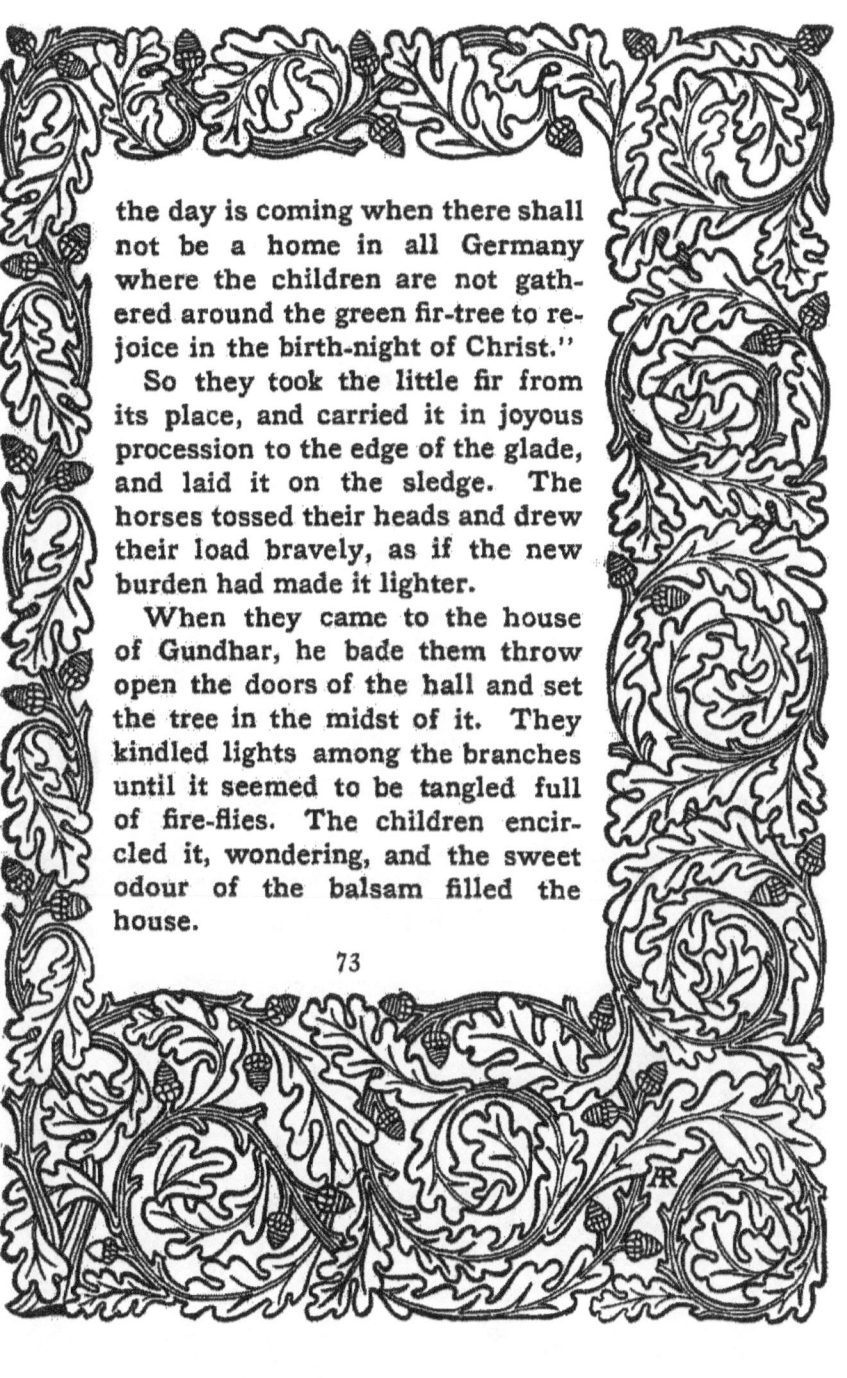

the day is coming when there shall
not be a home in all Germany
where the children are not gathered around the green fir-tree to re-
joice in the birth-night of Christ.''

So they took the little fir from
its place, and carried it in joyous
procession to the edge of the glade,
and laid it on the sledge. The
horses tossed their heads and drew
their load bravely, as if the new
burden had made it lighter.

When they came to the house
of Gundhar, he bade them throw
open the doors of the hall and set
the tree in the midst of it. They
kindled lights among the branches
until it seemed to be tangled full
of fire-flies. The children encir-
cled it, wondering, and the sweet
odour of the balsam filled the
house.

73

Then Winfried stood beside the chair of Gundhar, on the daïs at the end of the hall, and told the story of Bethlehem; of the babe in the manger, of the shepherds on the hills, of the host of angels and their midnight song. All the people listened, charmed into stillness.

But the boy Bernhard, on Irma's knee, folded by her soft arm, grew restless as the story lengthened, and began to prattle softly at his mother's ear.

"Mother," whispered the child, "why did you cry out so loud, when the priest was going to send me to Valhalla?"

"Oh, hush, my child," answered the mother, and pressed him closer to her side.

"Mother," whispered the boy again, laying his finger on the

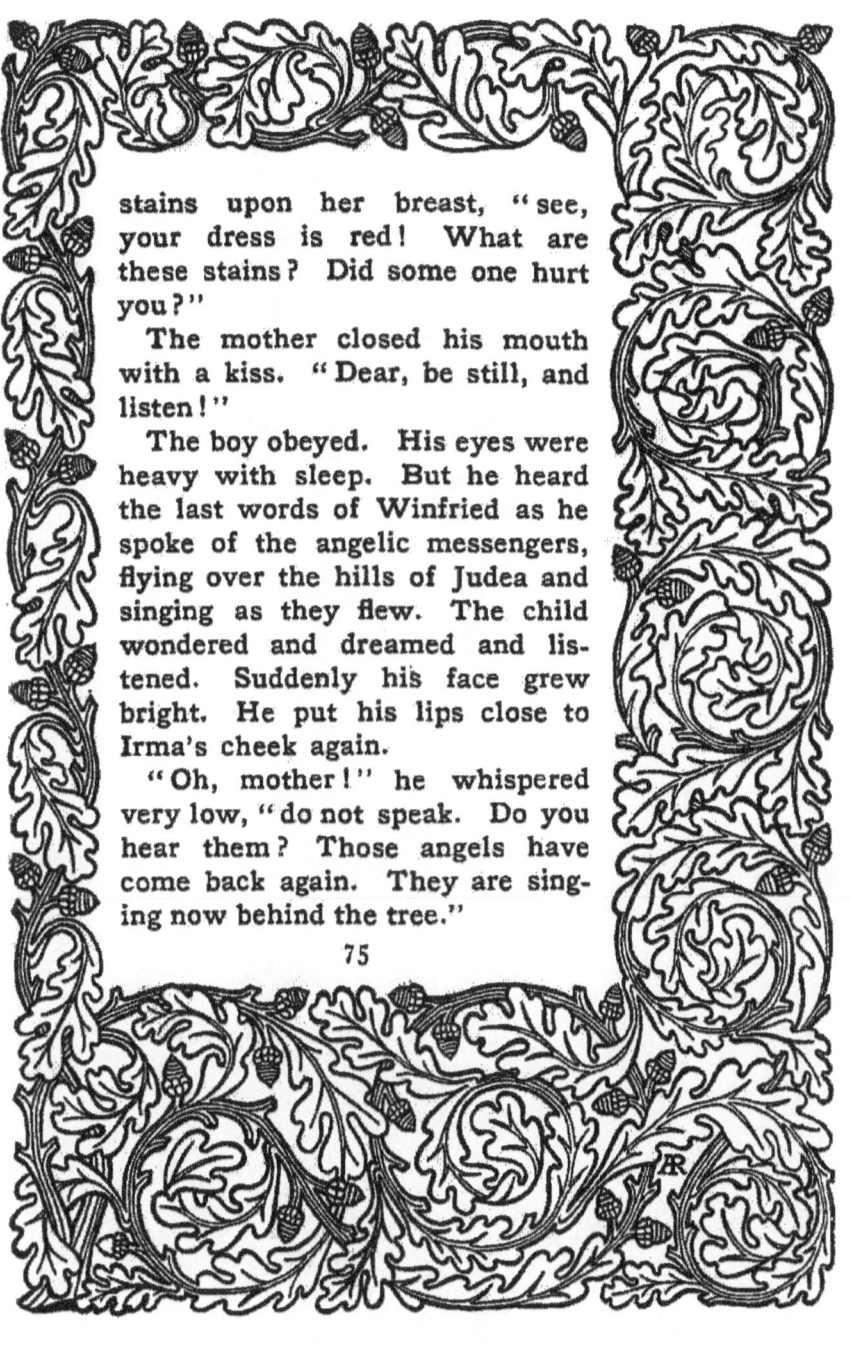

stains upon her breast, "see, your dress is red! What are these stains? Did some one hurt you?"

The mother closed his mouth with a kiss. "Dear, be still, and listen!"

The boy obeyed. His eyes were heavy with sleep. But he heard the last words of Winfried as he spoke of the angelic messengers, flying over the hills of Judea and singing as they flew. The child wondered and dreamed and listened. Suddenly his face grew bright. He put his lips close to Irma's cheek again.

"Oh, mother!" he whispered very low, "do not speak. Do you hear them? Those angels have come back again. They are singing now behind the tree."

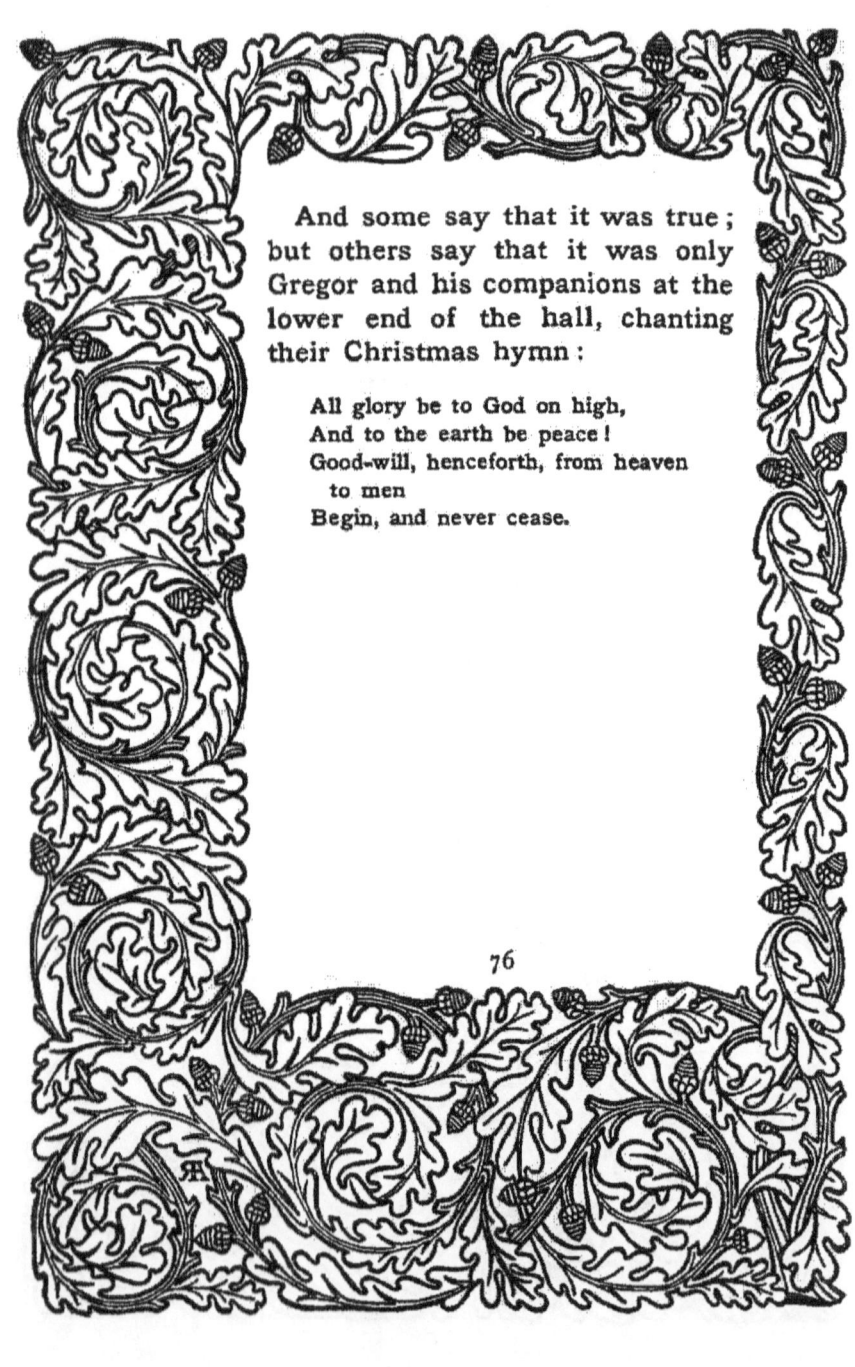

And some say that it was true;
but others say that it was only
Gregor and his companions at the
lower end of the hall, chanting
their Christmas hymn :

All glory be to God on high,
And to the earth be peace!
Good-will, henceforth, from heaven
  to men
Begin, and never cease.

76